City of Runaways

Delia Simpson

Cover Illustration: Keegan Blazey
Editor: Ana Joldes

ISBN-13: 9798648177352

Contents

1. Crude Subtlety.................................1

2. Wooden Dreams..............................14

3. The Runaways.................................27

4. A Bath in Suspicious Vibrations...........44

5. The End of a Movement.....................58

6. Oblivious Co-operation......................75

7. Claustrophobia and Other Conditions......86

8. Shove. Gasp..................................100

9. In the Manner of............................118

10. Coda...139

One – Crude Subtlety

N o matter how hard Herb tried, the grass never seemed to get any shorter. He stood in his field after a long day's work, the autumn-burnt blades reaching up to his chest. He'd spend hours at a time cutting and mowing, but no matter what he did, it always remained the same length. Mowing, mowing and mowing all day with his mechanical mower and it never made a difference. That's how he introduced himself to new people—'The mower that keeps on mowing because the grass just keeps on growing.' He didn't have many friends.

As Herb was mowing his way through the field, he found himself at the humble wood hut he'd built there. He'd wanted to use it as storage, but ever since the great sheep infestation of the year 379-Grape-3, he'd had to rent it out to a local inventor just to make ends meet. He kept a variety of lawnmowers in the kitchen instead.

The small hut was exuding smoke and muffling the metallic clang of Bell-tech® hammers, Diaphragm & Sons™ saws and drills, and Arson Incorporated® welding torches. Now, as the raucous racket rattled through his ears, he was regretting renting the tools out too.

His first impression of Rocket was that she was clearly a genius. When he'd asked her what she would be using the hut for, she'd replied with 'deuterium flow regulators through a magnetic assembly...' but he'd stopped listening by that point.

Not for the first time, Herb was concerned for the welfare of his property. *What did she actually make in there?* He got closer to the hut, his footsteps more than drowned out by the welding torch Rocket had started using.

Suddenly, the welding stopped. Herb froze.

With a smash and a clunk, a large metal object came hurtling through the window and landed with a dull thud at Herb's feet. A few inches closer and his toes would have been more familiar with the ground than he would have liked.

Herb kneeled in front of the object and analysed it closely. The metal pipes and curves formed the workings of a combustion engine, but there was something more to it. The golden sheen and the warm eminence of a fresh weld divided the engine into two distinct segments. He looked closer, the letter 'R' was engraved on the side. It was Rocket's trademark symbol, same as the one flashing and sparking above the hut door in a nauseating variety of neon colours.

A feeling of dread overcame Herb, as if pressing further would lead to something best left untouched. He raised his fist to knock, imagining a whole world of potential adventure and infinite possibilities awaiting him beyond the door. All that power in a fist: *Terrifying.* Not wishing to know more for the sake of his own sanity, Herb lowered his fist and went back to his mowing, blissfully ignorant of the true future he'd avoided, pitying any poor soul who'd have the courage to knock.

#

That was the fourth hybrid combustion engine this week that had managed to find its way out of the window. Rocket didn't know how they did it, but it seemed to happen a lot. One minute they were on one side of the window, the next they were on the other. She was sure that her throwing them in the general direction of the window had nothing to do with it, and the fact that the thin layer of glass that separated her from the outside world always ended up shattered on the floor at approximately the same time was a completely unrelated side effect.

Whilst considering this, Rocket had taken an iron cog from a wooden chest and hammered it in place in a large complicated machine that took up the entirety of the left-hand wall of her hut.

Some final checks before the first test of her invention:

Cogs interlocking—check.

Induction sequencer welded to the phase monitor—check.

Flux capaci—*Nah, no need to check that, it'd probably work.*

Rocket was so confident it was going to work this time that she took off her protective goggles and let down her chin-length hair. She'd started tying it up after the fourth time one of her inventions exploded and caught fire; this time, it was definitely, definitely, *definitely* not going to explode. But it didn't feel right. Suddenly deciding that she *did* in fact want her invention to explode, she reapplied her goggles and tied her hair back up again.

All checks complete; it was time to switch it on. She grabbed hold of a cable that was trailing along the floor and followed it away from the end that was connected to her atrocity of a machine. No button. She dug around in the lint-ridden, trinket-stuffed pockets of her dirty white and green lab coat and found a small one. With one quick blast of her blowtorch, she connected the button to the cable.

Before she'd even fully pressed it, a forceful jet of steam propelled Rocket across the hut. She clattered against the far wall, knocking over some scrap metal that had been innocently resting on a shelf. The room exploded into chaos. Cogs and pipes flew everywhere. The newest metal cog snapped off and jammed itself into the wooden wall of the hut, right where Rocket's face had been moments earlier. Thankfully, Rocket had the innate reflexes of a Tirollian panda bear and was particularly adept at dodging small projectiles. The right side of the machine exploded, completely obliterating the remaining windows that hadn't already been smashed by the rogue combustion engine minutes earlier.

A copy of *City, The Curious* got blown straight into her face. Well, being surrounded by chaos was as good a time to read the news as any. The front-page article, authored by Mattai Morieux advertised a brand new diagonal apartment block in the city. She flicked through the inner pages, ignoring the fact that a stray sheet of metal had just annihilated her toolbox. Apparently the bi-monthly clockwork poker final was to be held at the amphitheatre next week, 500 more people had been provisioned for the Blue Guard, and the Beirasmus market was to be extended by another week following a disastrous seahawk attack the other day. Oh, and the value of Honeywax had dropped again.

Rocket dropped her newspaper and sighed as a screw whizzed past her left ear. For some reason, the fact that creating dangerous fire and explosion-prone inventions in a wooden hut may be a slight safety hazard had never occurred to her. Instead, she seemed perfectly content to grab the nearest fire extinguisher and blast out the flames that were now consuming most of the roof.

Finally deciding to try to control the situation, Rocket grabbed one of her Bell-tech® hammers from the tool stand in the corner and tossed it between the two wheels that were spinning more and more violently. Smoke engulfed the hut as the machine juddered to a grinding halt and she coughed trying to wave it out of her face.

She tapped her home-made fire extinguisher twice to thank it for its service. It was the last thing she had made in her old workshop before it burned down. Why people laughed whenever she told the story, she had no idea.

She looked around her hut, observing the results of the latest disaster. It was perfection—the exact type of retirement she'd wanted. Rocket wasn't old, but she'd received a generous amount of hush money from a recent project and had decided to use it the only way she knew how. *A retirement isn't a retirement if it doesn't involve explosions.* But it felt like something was missing. Sure, building random machines and watching them blow up was fun, but she craved an opportunity to make something that worked. The problem was that she couldn't for the life of her decide what that could be. She'd tried to build a steam-powered stovepipe, but halfway through had decided that even that would look better flying across the room in a million pieces than above her head. If someone were to turn up and present her with a wonderfully crazy and ambitious idea right at this very moment, it might just bring her out of retirement.

Suddenly, there was a knock on the door, then another, then another. Rocket thought it was probably Herb the farmer coming over to complain about the noise. She'd ignore it until he went away.

Knock, knock, knock.

Rocket rolled her eyes and went over to the door where a plethora of locks kept it firmly shut. Perhaps she could convince him to play clockwork poker with her? She really craved a game right now. *Damn journalists and their advertising techniques.*

She fetched a set of rustic keys from a drawer under her worktop and made a few attempts at finding the right one before the lock beneath the handle clicked. She reached up to the top of the door and slid along a bolt, then knelt down right at the base of the door and slid another bolt the other way. Finally, she tapped in a four-digit code—7334—on a keypad created from the keys of an old typewriter. A little red light on the pad went green.

She took off her protective black leather gloves and placed her thumb on a plate to the left of the door; a little red light next to that went green also.

She counted to three. The door clicked open.

#

There was so much on the line, and Galileo was nervous.

'Can't even chart a simple constellation!' had been the review on his latest paper; he'd show them. 'His words are as empty, void and lacking in life as a black hole!' had been the heckle at his talk at the latest monthly guild dinner, much to the enjoyment of his colleagues, who'd shown their appreciation by incongruously striking their glasses of ginger crush with their eating utensils; he'd show them. Galileo was clever, and he knew that, but he struggled to accept that he was not the most competent talker. Writing things was tough too. He much preferred to draw diagrams, explain with equations, and plan with paintings.

Unfortunately for him, his negative reviews had not gone unnoticed, and the guild had had enough. He couldn't bear the thought of being kicked out, but that's what they'd threatened. He'd dedicated his whole life to searching the stars for knowledge, so without it, he'd be nothing. It angered him deeply that the accuracy and quality of his findings meant less to the guild than their public image, but there were no other organisations with the resources and the Honeywax that Galileo needed for his ambitious research projects. He'd defend his post there to the end. He had to make this work.

His few supporters at the Astronomers' Guild had each given their suggestions on which inventor Galileo should enlist the help of, if he was to succeed in his most recent wild goose chase. Unfortunately, every single one of them had been mysteriously unavailable.

Galileo found himself in a field, just outside a small wooden hut, surrounded by exceptionally large blades of grass which clawed at his brown frock coat. *Someone really ought to mow this*, he thought to himself. He checked a piece of paper that had the address written on it. It was different from her last hut and the thought of what must have happened to it didn't fill him with optimism.

He only ever went to Rocket when he absolutely needed to. He thought she was clever, brilliant and passionate, if not difficult to work with at times. The guild would often joke that if anyone ever suggested an impossibly ambitious project that was doomed to fail, they should go to Rocket for help. Even so, Galileo was young and ambitious enough that he couldn't help smiling at the prospect of proposing the proposal he was about to propose. He was blatantly aware of the grin on his face but could do nothing to conceal it as Rocket began to open the door. He could hear every click and tap of the key, and with each one, his heart beat a little faster. He could imagine what the expression on her face would be when she realised it was him on the other side. He was reminded of his competitors at the Astronomers' Guild, and how they'd ridiculed him when he'd claimed he was going to be the first person to complete maps and charts of the entire world. He couldn't help but be reminded of their cynical faces in a circle around him, and how they'd pushed him between them, laughing.

'Alright then, Gally—20,000 Honeywax says you can't!' the ringleader had bet as she'd prodded her thumb into his shoulder, forcing him up against the wall, terrified. His smile vanished in a wave of anxiety as he remembered the experience and how horrible it had felt, but then, that's what all this was about. He'd sunk everything he had into this, so he had to get it right first time. Galileo doubted his bullies would pay up, but that wasn't the point; he was the kind of person who, when his heart was set on something, would never give up on achieving his goals, even if it was just to prove a point. He cared more about his guild membership than the money, but it'd be nice to show them he was capable. He forced the smile back and the thoughts out of his head.

He desperately needed Rocket's help, but he knew she was volatile and would likely be the cause of many a stressful evening. But she was the only one who would do it. Potentially she was the only one crazy enough to be capable of doing it. He scratched his head, foreshadowing his own headaches. He needed to say something. The clicking of the locks had ceased seconds ago. He panicked. Words stopped. His mind raced at a million knots, trying to think of something to say over the murky fog of his own thoughts. *Why was talking so difficult?*

\#

'Oh, it's you,' Rocket said, deadpan. 'Sorry, I'm retired.'

She attempted to close the door as quickly as it had opened, but by the time she'd shut it, Galileo had already sidestepped inside. It took Rocket a good few seconds to notice that he was standing right behind her. She typed in a code on a keypad to the right of the door, took off her left boot and raised her toe to the plate on the left of the door, slid the bolts at the top and the bottom of the door back into place, and finally found the right key in the set to re-lock the door with.

'What do *you* want?' asked Rocket, wanting only to be left alone with her explosions. Galileo replied by taking off his knapsack and unrolling several scrolls out onto the only clear part of Rocket's worktop.

Galileo beckoned her over before he began talking at speed and length about the tablecloth of parchment. He talked through various equations, lists, diagrams, graphs and charts, but there was something about Galileo's voice when talking about his theories that made Rocket want to fall asleep. She was more of a practical person. She'd just nod and agree at the end and hope that she hadn't just agreed to something really dull and boring, or worse, something that didn't involve a welding torch. Maybe she could even fit in a quick weld or two before he finally finished talking.

Rocket turned her back on him, went back to her invention on the wall and started hammering in one of the cogs that had sprung out. She knew Galileo was artistic. His list of skills apart from maths, astronomy and physics included music, painting and poetry, and she could have sworn that some of the equations he was spouting out at break-neck speed rhymed, possibly even following iambic pentameter. Her very first tutor had insisted that poetry and physics were basically the same thing, and it was only now that she understood why.

Unfortunately, Rocket had forgotten that a finely tuned peripheral vision was also one of Galileo's skills. That, along with the raucous racket of wrenching had alerted him to the fact that she was not listening to him.

He insisted that Rocket just come and have a look at some of the charts, blatantly frustrated at her lack of interest. She finally complied, quickly scanned the documents, mumbled 'whatever,' and turned around... She quickly did a double-take, realising there was something missing, and a pattern. Her eyes darted left, right, up, down, left again, right again, before Rocket finally saw what she thought she didn't see. A map. An unfinished map. Star charts. Unfinished star charts. Everything was unfinished.

'They're not done?' she asked, instantly regretting taking his bait.

'Here...' he said, shifting the maps and charts to one side and unrolling a piece of blue parchment over the top. Rocket saw designs for a ship. It was a magnificent ship which Galileo had named the 'Leisurely Ländler' and that would be far bigger than any ship in the harbour should someone be mad enough to build it. It might even work. It might even be capable of going around the world, something that, to the best of her knowledge, had never been successfully attempted before. The thought sent such a shock of excitement up her spine that it caused her to bite her lip not to let it show. With all the subtlety of an Urban Wood-Bovine (not to be confused with the *Rural* Wood-Bovine which are notorious for their extreme and crude subtlety), she grabbed some cloth from a drawer in her worktop and placed it to her reddened mouth.

'Go on…' said Rocket muffled by the cloth as she leant against the wall like nothing had happened, feigning disinterest.

This time, though, she listened intently as Galileo talked about his plan to explore the world and to complete his maps and charts. He couldn't do it alone though. He came to Rocket for help with building the ship and to request that she be the captain. He'd planned out everything immaculately down to the very last detail. He showed her prospective routes and potential locations to visit— his markings looked artistic. Rocket's second tutor had always insisted that geography and painting were basically the same thing, but this had been obvious to Rocket from the beginning.

She didn't care about the routes or the locations. Her inner child was screaming at this opportunity—to be able to build a ship of her own design, capable of crossing oceans and to command it herself. She could be a great adventurer. *Rocket: Explorer Extraordinaire.* She imagined herself sailing the seas, a brilliant buccaneer. It was a dream come true. She remembered articles in *City, The Curious* about a group of artists who'd gone into self-imposed exile hundreds of years ago. No one had heard from them since. The article had implied that they were killed, but Rocket had always wondered if that really was the truth. Now, she could find out.

She was fairly certain she could get away with her own interpretation of Galileo's blueprints. It was even better that it was a vehicle; something that she could constantly be tinkering with to improve. Forget explosions, this was the real deal. On the inside, she was jumping up and down with anticipation—finally a project she could really sink her teeth into. She was so excited she could... she could...

'Yeah, seems okay. Why me?' she asked, feeling the need to draw out her answer.

'You're...' Galileo stuttered, struggling for words. 'The only one who could do it.'

Now that was what she wanted to hear. With her ego fully boosted and having led Galileo on for long enough, she agreed to take the job. She offered a hand to him which he reluctantly took. The deal and their partnership were sealed, and the journey of a lifetime was only just beginning.

'Just don't use the colour green,' said Galileo. 'You know I can't stand green.'

Two – Wooden Dreams

S he was different. No one else was quite *this* different, which is why the people of the city had all unanimously decided that she was different. Sure, the city was filled with a variety of people, all various races, religions, backgrounds, sizes and finger-nail lengths, but Veroushka was different because she was made of wood.

As she sat at one of the outside tables of her usual café, 'The Canary', looking up at the stars and drinking her jasmine tea, she was blissfully unaware of the passers-by, who would stare at her unusual bright white and red barky complexion and point at the magical strings that controlled her twiggy fingers.

She was trying to spot *constellations*, a word she'd only just learnt at the latest talk at the Astronomers' Guild. The word sounded good in her head, like she'd heard it before but couldn't remember where from. She loved those talks and couldn't wait for the next one, especially since it was due to be given by the one that spoke in rhymes.

Despite her sheltered life, Veroushka had done quite well for herself. She was able to enjoy cups of tea at the local café in as much harmony as the busy cobbled streets of the city would allow, especially this late in the evening. Her unique biological make-up allowed her to savour liquids, but she was simply unable to consume solid foods. Except for cake. Cake was okay. *Chocolate and matcha cheesecake went well with jasmine tea*, she thought, making a mental note to order this combination again next time. The effort that went into using her magical strings to carefully descend the fork to the plate, press down hard enough to cut a slice and lift it back up to her mouth, made the result of this delicate operation even more worthwhile. The marionette was probably more capable of appreciating tea and cake than anyone else in the city.

Catching sight of a waiter, she let him know that the cake was one of the most delicious treats she'd ever tasted. It was sweet, delicate and refreshing, and she thought it suited her. The waiter informed her that it was a home-made recipe invented by their chef and that he would pass on the compliments to her.

The town square was clearing. The people all seemed to be walking in one direction. Veroushka had read in her copy of *City,*

The Curious earlier that a fairground had opened up nearby, so she guessed this was where they were all going. Deciding that it might be a good idea to do the same, she finished the last of her tea as quickly as she dared, left some Honeywax coins on the table and prepared to go. *Allons-y.* With a jolt, her right foot raised up off the ground revealing her shiny red satin shoes and long white tights. With a second jolt, her right arm followed, thrusting her whole body up to reveal her white top and red velvet coat with golden tassels on the arms. Her whole body seemed to hover in mid-air for a fraction of a second before slowly descending to the ground, her long pink and blue striped skirt flowing down to rest against her knobbly knees a moment later.

A string guided down her left hand to the table and her hands clenched around her newspaper so that she could lift it up and hold it close. The strings guided her feet, one in front of the other, like a child learning to walk for the first time. Of course, people stared, but she just ignored it.

It didn't take long for Veroushka to find the queues to enter the fairground, she just had to follow the crowd after all. They were split into three, so after careful deliberation, Veroushka decided to go for the middle one. As she approached, the middle queue split and merged into the two outer queues, leaving the way forward for her. Veroushka thought they were being kind, but they didn't return her smiles.

She approached the ticket booth, but before she could even say anything, the automated fair-teller was already excitedly welcoming her to the fairground in a high-pitched voice, like a children's hand puppet.

'Hi there, stranger. Welcome to the night fair!' it said, as the cogs under its little pedestal caused it to spin and jump around. *Incroyable!* 'Entry will cost ya three Honeywax and you get a freeee stamp, so you can come back in any old time you like. Just place your coins into the compartment below!' Veroushka giggled at the delightful teller as it went idle. Automation was the closest thing she had to a friend. She did as it instructed, following a neon sign down to a box in which she placed her money. A whoosh of air sucked up the coins. They rattled through the metal pipes. The teller sprang to life again as red and green lights flashed by its sides and a fanfare played. A mechanical arm sprouted from the teller's cage holding a stamp. Veroushka put her arm underneath and the stamp was pressed down on her gently, as the ink started dripping off her wooden skin, down her fingers, and onto the ground.

'Wahooo!' the teller shouted. 'Please, make your way through the turnstile and enjoy your visit!' The teller finally shut down as Veroushka's strings lifted her over the turnstile and into the night fair.

Now, she could go anywhere. The lights and sounds of the night fair overwhelmed Veroushka as she looked around. Would she go to the giant teacups that were spinning round and round with children screaming in them? No, she was too refined for something like that. Would she get babarak candy from the stall? No, she couldn't eat solid foods. She could have her photo taken by the nice-looking photographer. That thought appealed to her and she imagined having a self-portrait hanging over her tiny little fireplace in her tiny little home. A feeling of sadness always came over Veroushka as she imagined her home. Really, it was just a place of temporary residence. It was her dream to find her *real* home. She'd never had her photo taken before, *c'est super!* But no, she didn't want a crowd of fair-goers staring at her more than they already were. Instead, Veroushka resigned herself to wandering around aimlessly and simply taking in the sights, sounds and smells.

She walked over to where a large crowd was gathered in a circle. Naturally, they moved away from her, allowing her to reach the front where two dancers posed, waiting for their cue. It came moments later as a soft jazzy tune and the two dancers smoothly twirled and spun around each other. The crowd clapped on the off-beat, so Veroushka joined in, cheering them on and enjoying the romantic spectacle. After the performance finished, Veroushka tried her best to jump up and down with excitement and clap as fast as she could, giddy, as the crowd dispersed around her. *Encore!*

She looked around again, where to next?

In a less crowded corner of the fair, a lone performer in long flared trousers and a purple waistcoat was preparing some plates next to a peculiar contraption. *Déroutante!* Veroushka wandered over. The device was long, had a seat at one end and a big wheel at the other. What could this performer possibly do with this device and a stack of plates? Her question was soon answered as he balanced the plates on a pole, climbed aboard his unicycle, and steadied himself back and forth before placing the pole on his nose so that the plates were now four feet in the air above him.

Magnifique! He dropped his pole and plates onto the floor and steadied himself again. This time, he picked up four skittles and juggled them, staring up at them as they flipped over his head. *Plus magnifique!* The performer hopped off his unicycle and bowed to Veroushka, once again giddy with excitement.

With a massive grin painted onto her barky white face, Veroushka looked around once more, her sight returning to the teacups, spinning and moving around in a circle at the same time. *Très nauséeux.* She hadn't wanted to do that earlier, but now, with a taste for adventure… she simply had to try it!

She approached the front of the queue, which mysteriously vanished in her presence and asked politely for the guard to let her in. He instantly held out a hand and shook his head, blocking her way. Veroushka was confused, but the guard tapped a sign to his right, pointing out a figure with a horizontal line drawn above its head. She was smaller than even most of the children, so health and safety prevented her from going on the ride.

She bowed her head to the floor and walked away with her upside-down smile. She realised that she was alone; everyone else had come to the fair with someone else, nobody wanted to be near her and she wasn't even allowed on any rides. *C'est tellement frustrant!*

Ça suffit! It didn't take long for Veroushka to find the exit to the fairground. Disappointed and alone, she left.

#

The label on her red leather jacket read 'Vale,' so this is what people called her when they approached her to ask for a photo. It was a somewhat embarrassing name, but she was content with it. Much to her disappointment, when you took up a part-time job as a photographer at the local night fair, people would approach you and ask you for things. She had to pay rent on her small apartment somehow though. This was half the job she'd trained for, so it would do for now.

After two hours of taking pictures of strangers, she was hungry, thirsty and had a headache. *Half an hour left.*

Next in the queue was a family of five. The kids stared for a second at the strange attire of the lady standing in front of them— dark-red, tattered, leather jacket with a white shirt and waistcoat underneath. She wore a red cap, ripped black trousers and a bow tie. In this city, poor people stuck out like a sore thumb. The kids' parents shuffled them in front of a big grey screen that Vale had set up in a quieter section of the fair and Vale asked what background they'd like. After careful consideration, they decided to go for the cowboy-themed backdrop. Vale lifted a film canister from a trunk and placed it into a large wooden projector that was facing the screen and switched it on.

Spending so much time at the fair, Vale was used to seeing lots of people, but as she turned around to pick up her camera, she noticed strange strings coming down from the sky, and at their other end, someone different. The bumbling little marionette was wandering over in her direction. Instinctively, Vale wanted to talk to her, ask her about her life. *What was it like being different? What did she like doing?* She wanted to find out everything about her. But as the marionette placed her newspaper on the table nearby and walked off into the crowd, she remembered that she had a job to do.

She looked down at the newspaper the marionette had left. The traditional dark-blue print on cream paper was familiar to her as *City, The Curious*, a paper which she often did small bits of work for, but these jobs were few and far between. She tried to focus on her job but couldn't help catching sight of the front page, advertising an article on city architecture, authored by one *Mattai Morieux*. Vale was all too aware of his success and was definitely not jealous in any way.

Nope.

Not jealous at all. Not after they'd gone to study journalism together, worked on projects together, and certainly not after he'd thrown her under the bus to work full-time for the biggest paper in the city, without so much as a goodbye. She felt her face turn red hot with not jealousy.

She flipped over the newspaper so that she wouldn't have to look at her rival's article and aimed her camera at the family, who were now growing restless and impatient.

She gestured to the family to move slightly to the left before looking down the lens. She twisted a dial on the side to alter the focus, and another to alter the exposure. It was a fairly old camera, a vintage, passed down for generations, but wasn't worth much. It did the job though and Vale took it everywhere she went.

Her finger pressed down the small circular button on the top of the camera, and, with a flash, the photo was taken.

After another hour of the repetitive cycle of setting up a family in front of the screen, taking a picture, printing it off and giving it to them, Vale finally locked off the end of the queue, apologised to the customers remaining and packed up her camera. She'd stayed late, just to get an extra few Honeywax for her morning mug of meyacot.

The constant fairground music in the background had been an earworm in her brain. Her headache worsened. Vale clutched at her forehead as if trying to physically remove the tune from her memory. It didn't help of course, but she found comfort in the fact she was about to leave.

She slung her camera case over her shoulder and took one last look around the fairground for the little marionette that had piqued her curiosity earlier, but she was lost in the crowd.

As she left the night fair, she considered *City, The Curious* once more. She'd grown up with it. Everyone had. It was how she'd learnt of the history of her city and how it became the place that it was today. She found it fascinating how a war, so long ago, had all but devastated civilisation, leaving only remnants of their technology behind. The city was in a good place now having mostly recovered but it was still a long way away from what it used to be. That was how *City, The Curious* encouraged the population of the city, by motivating them to strive to make the city as great as it once was.

Although she believed most of it, Vale was cynical enough to realise that the paper was the only source of news available and the entire population had no choice other than to believe the little scraps of information that it offered them. After all, there was no one left alive to remember it. The real history of the city was probably lost forever. The version Vale knew was likely not too far from the truth though, and it did explain the mix of lowly clockwork, mechanical and steam technology with the seemingly impossible.

Not long after she'd graduated with Mattai, they'd taken a trip to the City Museum, back when they'd been inseparable friends. They'd been in awe of some of the ancient quills on display. Automatic ink refills and predictive word completion being some of the many intricate features they'd boasted. Nowadays, one could only acquire working ancient tech from the black market, at a price higher than the amount of Honeywax Vale had earned over the course of her entire life.

She supposed that the paper did suit the city, what with it being the only paper people read and the city being the only place where people lived. It was *just* the city. There was nowhere else. Well, there were the bandit towns in the desert, but they didn't count. From what she'd heard, the towns were tiny, and the people who resided there lived like scavengers. Then again, she'd read that in *City, The Curious,* so she had no idea how accurate this was.

She'd lived in the city her whole life and always dreamt of somewhere else. She didn't even know what somewhere else looked like, but had such a vivid imagination that her competence for inventing her own *somewhere else* had been her gateway into journalism. How people got by without dreaming of somewhere else was beyond her. She found herself drawn to the idea that whatever she wrote in *City, The Curious* would be read and believed by everyone.

Vale kept herself going with the thought that one day she would be out there, somewhere else, taking pictures of the world, doing some real journalism and knowing that the entire city was looking at her work. She would be discovering new things and showing them to the world, not just showing off some buildings and inventing stories like Mattai Morieux. As the sounds and smells of the fair faded from her ears and nose, she sighed.

Her work for the night was far from over.

#

Vale worked alone in her apartment on the 37th floor of a 38-story wooden skyscraper, processing the pictures she'd taken throughout the week. It was small, cramped and dusty, but about as much as a struggling freelance photojournalist could afford in a city like this. She'd hoped that being so high up would mean she could at least get a good view, but the only thing she could see out of the window was the 37th floor apartment of the wooden skyscraper next door. In fact, right now, she couldn't even see that. She'd converted her entire apartment into a darkroom photography studio, so black visors blocked all light from coming in. A thin veil of dark red light allowed her to see what she was doing.

Carefully, she used a pair of tweezers to immerse a fresh piece of printing paper in developer chemicals, admiring and considering her own work as it shimmered in the liquid. She was able to print drafts directly from her vintage camera, but the result was never as good as the real thing. She could use these properly processed pictures, however, to get herself some work.

She quickly removed the print from the chemicals and used her free hand to balance the other edge as she moved it into the final chemical bath. This was the last picture she needed to develop, so she went over to the window, pulled on a chord and opened the blinds. She was surprised to see the sun already rising and the dawn light flooding in—had she really been working this late? She yawned. A big yawn. It hurt her jaw.

She stared out of the window at the neighbouring apartment, looked up, down and off to the side. A wooden jungle. It made for good photography, but it did get old after a while. What she really wanted was to be able to take pictures of new things, exciting things, wonderful things. She wanted to expose everyone to a world outside the walls of the wooden city. *There must be so much more the world has to offer beyond this boring wooden life*, she thought. Vale refused to believe that this was all there was: wake up, take pictures, develop pictures, sleep.

Vale yawned again. There was, however, one last thing she needed to do. A letter. She'd made herself promise that she'd write it, finally removing herself from those toxic part-time jobs at *City, The Curious* and ridding herself of Mattai Morieux once and for all. She sat down at her small wooden desk and slipped a piece of printing paper under one of the feet to stop it from wobbling as she aggressively typed out her letter. Finally, she was going to give a piece of her mind to the editor. Of course, this was going to mean she needed to find some other way of earning money. There were no other newspapers, so it would be difficult. Historically, other newspapers had mysteriously vanished in under a month, but maybe she'd get lucky and write for her own travel column? She'd need some way of travelling the world, but that was the Vale of tomorrow's problem.

With an incredibly vague plan in mind, she finished off her angry letter, climbed into her slightly uncomfortable bed, and didn't sleep a wink.

Three – The Runaways

Runaway: a place where outcasts from the city lived. The sign at the entrance indicated that it had a population of just 32. The city proper was so far away that its tall wooden skyscrapers and surrounding metal walls were just about visible on the horizon. A long strip of desert separated Runaway from its much, much larger brother.

Folks in Runaway stuck together. It was a tight but friendly and welcoming community. They all had a common enemy to fear: the Blue Guard. If it wasn't for them, the townspeople would still be living their normal lives with their normal families in the big city.

Instead, they made do with their Runaway lives and their Runaway families.

Eliza was the first. She founded the town over 40 years ago and continued to serve as its sheriff and mayor to this day. She insisted the townsfolk call her Eliza, but they had too much respect for her. Only Sheriff Eliza would do. She had kept them safe from bandits as well as the Blue Guard for many a year. They had faith in her, even in her old age.

Sheriff Eliza lay unconscious in Doc Holliday's medical practice, the fourth building on the right of the only street in town. They called it Runway. She'd broken into a bandit camp to the north to retrieve an old family heirloom that had been stolen in the night from one of the new, naïve runaways who hadn't thought to hide their valuables. She came out with a bullet in the leg for her troubles, and the heirloom, of course. Holliday had given her a home-brew sedative so that she wouldn't feel it when he removed the bullet.

The first chime of the clock tower caused Holliday to nearly drop the bullet from his tweezers as he transferred it from Eliza's leg to a glass jar on his worktop. *8 seconds to noon.*

Holliday pressed a button on the auto-doc above to complete the stitching and removed his white mask and apron, hanging them up on a stand by the window. As he looked out, he thought he could see something in the desert, approaching Runaway with haste. It was probably nothing. The Blue Guard often scouted that area making sure none of the runaways made it back into the city, not that it made a difference.

He looked through some of his cupboards and took down various bottles of liquid, plant extracts, herbal remedies and other natural formulae. He took a syringe from a tray near the operating table and filled it with the remaining liquid from the only bottle that had anything in it. The second chime from the clock tower caused Holliday to nearly drop this too. *7 seconds to noon.*

As Holliday prepared a solution for the old sheriff, he heard gunshots coming from outside. The Blue Guard after a new runaway no doubt. Holliday sincerely hoped they made it to the town. With the liquid prepared, he injected it into Eliza's arm; she'd be right as rain in a couple of hours. He took his stethoscope and checked for a heartbeat. Rumour had it, he'd once had an important life to save, say, someone high up in the Blue Guard, and maybe, just maybe it hadn't quite worked out. Maybe that was why he was a runaway. No one could prove it. He always checked to make sure his patients were alive since the day that event may or may not have happened.

The third chime. *6 seconds to noon.* Seconds always seemed to go slower the closer they got to noon. No one knew why.

The gunshots were getting closer... *odd.* If it was a new runaway, the Blue Guard would have given up this close to the town. Holliday went to the window and looked into the yellow sea. It wasn't the Blue Guard at all, it was a group of bandits. Only three of them. *Idiots couldn't track bovine through sand. This ought to be fun*, he thought to himself. Clearly, they were after the sheriff, but there wasn't a soul in Runaway that wouldn't give their life for Eliza. With only three of them though, none of the runaways needed to die today. Holliday'd take care of them himself. Fourth chime, *5 seconds to noon.*

Holliday grabbed his holster from a hat stand and tied it around his waist, picked up his revolver from the desk and fitted it into the straps. He knew it was loaded. He always kept it loaded. What else did he need? Stetson. With a single hand, he flipped it around and placed it on his head in unison with the fifth chime. *4 seconds to noon.*

The metal saloon doors opened automatically as Holliday approached them. The sandy street was deserted. The desert was not. Three masked bandits approached the entrance to the town, and, with a canister of red spray paint, one of them crossed out the number 32 on the sign and replaced it with a 31. They looked down Runway, metal buildings with corrugated metal roofs lined the street. At the other end, the metal town hall, the largest building, was almost certainly where their target was. The clock ticked over and a sixth chime rang out. *3 seconds to noon.*

The bandits dismounted from their clockwork horses, the whirring of their mechanical parts stopping a moment later. They used rope to tie them to the metal framework of the first building on Runway. Not that they would go anywhere, they were clockwork after all and didn't have a mind of their own. A different bandit took a cylindrical tool and used it to roll a poster up onto the metal building. It was a wanted poster, complete with a photograph of Sheriff Eliza and offering the reward of 'NOT DEATH' in return for her. Bandits always had the most attractive of reward offers. Holliday watched. It seemed pointless to him that they'd stick up that poster, considering they were looking for her themselves. What did bandits know though? The chimes rang out again, *2 seconds to noon.*

Holliday stood in the centre of the street, staring down towards the entrance. The three bandits stood at the opposite end, staring right back. Holliday was all that stood between them and the sheriff. As he watched them, he wondered what they thought about the town. Did they consider themselves honourable citizens, and Runaway a bandit camp? Holliday didn't suppose it mattered, the term 'bandit' was highly subjective, after all.

'Give us the sheriff. We'll leave quietly,' the leader of the three demanded, taking the straw from her mouth as her voice echoed off the metal buildings that surrounded her.

Holliday wasn't going to give in to the ultimatum. He stood his ground, staring more intently at them. He tipped the brim of his Stetson to protect his eyes from the intense burning of the sun. His hand hovered by his side and he exercised his fingers, poised to strike at any time. The three bandits did the same. *1 second to noon.*

Holliday's eyes narrowed. He analysed the position of the three bandits. His revolver was strapped on his left-hand side, so shooting them left to right would be most effective. The leader was the most important target though, so he could risk going for that one first. Not worth it, the time difference of shifting back slightly could be enough for them to get the upper hand. Distance between them—5 degrees, approximately. He worked out how much power he'd need to send to his wrist, and at what exact time he'd need to pull the trigger to hit all three as quickly as possible. The last chime of the clock should be happening right about...

Bong!

The sound of the gunshots echoed and reverberated off the corrugated metal rooftops. In Holliday's experience, dead people had worse reflexes than live ones. Being the forward-thinking doctor that he was, he didn't like to assume, but the fact that all three bandits now lay dead on Runway, proved his point. *More work for the undertaker... the economy is looking up,* he thought. He twirled his revolver on his finger and holstered it again, before returning to his medical practice.

#

The gleaming wheels and cogs of the horses pulled a black carriage up the gravel driveway of a large estate just outside the walls of the city. Inside, Leira and her parents stared out of the darkened windows at the biggest house they'd ever seen. To them, it was a castle.

Apart from the novelty of travelling in a carriage, the journey had been a boring one. The only points of interest had been a deserted fairground and an overgrown field, but Leira had kept herself somewhat entertained. She held a small black and gold device in her hand and flicked a rotary dial on it back and forth. It sent an electronic signal up the chord that connected it to the golden earpiece which was clipped to the side of her head. Cables and levers all worked together to propel sound into her ear at various frequencies. It was hidden underneath her hair—jet-black with intense, jagged, sea-blue highlights. Having coloured hair wasn't common. Leira liked hers well enough, but others weren't so lucky. A winged dial on the side of her music player turned up the volume as she twisted it clockwise.

The Šéf was a person that you were either incredibly happy or dreading to see. More often than not, both at the same time. Leira's parents were mostly dreading it. Leira herself mostly just wondered if the recruitment posters dotted around the city depicted him accurately. She was expecting a tall, thin man covered head to toe in golden blue, bejewelled robes with a dark-blue fez resting on his bald head. The Šéf controlled the Blue Guard, so naturally he was pretty much the most powerful person around. If you knew him personally, you either worked for him, or owed him something. The dashing figure in the pictures gleefully twirled his moustache as he beckoned people to join the provisioning ceremonies. Conveniently, Leira didn't know that the Šéf also led the black market in *people* and that girls with the hair colour genes often fetched a very high price, being so rare. Leira's parents had done their best to protect their 16-year-old daughter from him, but the promise of a good life was too tempting, even for them. They all went to the Šéf at some point. But this wasn't the Šéf's house, it was far too small for that. Currently, it was no one's house.

The carriage came to a stop in front of the large arches which formed the entrance to the house. The electronic doors slid open, and they were promptly greeted by the Šéf himself, arms wide open, smiling as always. He was far more overweight than the posters would have her believe. *What else about this man did she not know?* Gone was the golden cloak with colourful jewelled crests. Today, he was wearing his pin-striped suit, his mouth decorated with a clockwork cigar and body effervescing the stench of Honeywax. Today, he was on business.

'So glad you could make it!' he said to the parents, hugging each of them and kissing them on the cheek in turn. 'And I see you brought along the young one too! Finally came out of her bedroom, eh? Excellent!' he said looking straight at Leira with his eyebrows raised and a hearty chuckle. She didn't have her own bedroom, but in her experience rich men were always oblivious to what the unprivileged didn't have. Leira took off her earphones, nodded and smiled anyway, cringing internally. She didn't really want to be there, but then again, she didn't really want to be anywhere. Everywhere Leira went was *wrong*.

The Šéf's voice went low now, a cheeky low. 'Do you still want to come inside or have you... changed your mind?' he said, knowing full well they hadn't. It was their last chance to back out, but they'd come this far and already been seduced by the front entrance alone. Leira's parents turned to each other and slowly nodded. The Šéf's grin widened—they were locked in now. He held out a hand, guiding the small family into the house. In walked Leira's father, followed by her mother, Leira herself and behind her, the Šéf.

The reception of the mansion was bigger than their entire house in the city. A diamond chandelier hung above their heads, three staircases spiralled upwards and golden doors led off to the sides. The Šéf explained the history of the house, its original architects and how he had come to *acquire* it. Leira looked around but wasn't interested in his words, this still felt *wrong* to her.

The kitchens too were bigger than their house. She wondered if the bathroom was too. The Šéf explained that the larder was fully stocked, and a personal chef was ready to prepare any meal they wanted. Leira's ears perked up when she heard the mention of food.

A long rectangular table lined with plates and cutlery took up most of the dining room. On the walls hung animated portraits of who Leira imagined were important people. She didn't recognize any of them. Leira's parents looked at each other, happy and sad all at once.

Upstairs, the Šéf gave a tour of the bedrooms. There were three of them. The first had a giant king-sized bed with four posts. A big mirror, dressing table and an ornamented wooden cupboard that could easily hold the entire family's clothes three times over. The other two were slightly smaller—a colourful, sequinned bed throned in one and a cot in the other. Both were just as extravagant and would allow Leira a type of freedom she'd never known, but even so, it didn't feel right.

The quartet returned to the atrium, standing below the diamond chandelier.

'So, what do you think?' asked the Šéf, addressing the parents. Before they could answer, he took a puff of his clockwork cigar and quickly turned to Leira. 'Why don't you go wait in the carriage? There's a good girl.'

She didn't need to be asked twice. She walked outside and climbed into the carriage, resting on its soft leather seats and letting her short, sleeveless, ocean blue and white dress flow down over the chair. She clipped on her earpiece, selected a song and shut herself off. When she had her music on, the immersion in sound was as close to feeling right as she could find in the world.

Time passed.

More time passed.

Leira twisted the butterfly dial to turn up the volume further, drowning out the outside world entirely.

Suddenly, the carriage lurched forwards and Leira jumped with fright, the trotting of the mechanical horses speeding up bleeding through her music. The door slid open. Leira was expecting her parents. It wasn't them. If was the Šéf. He climbed in and shut the door behind him, turned to Leira and grinned his obnoxious grin in her face.

She twisted her body around, looking out of the back window as the mansion shrunk in the distance. She expected to see her parents running after the carriage. They were there alright, but they weren't running. They didn't even look concerned. They stared at the ground and shuffled their feet like naughty children who had just been told to think about what they'd done. But they daren't look up at the carriage that was taking their daughter away from them forever. They daren't even think about what was going to happen to her.

Leira hit the window with her fist as hard as she could, trying to get the attention of the people she had learnt to trust the most, but clearly the Šéf had done a good job of making sure that the carriage was sufficiently soundproof.

A hand rested on her left shoulder. If it wasn't her own hand, she didn't want it there. She only had to look down at it to see that it didn't connect to her own body. Leira wasn't an idiot, or naïve, she could guess what was happening. Stories of colour-haired girls disappearing forever weren't uncommon amongst her friends, but to her, they were just stories, until now at least.

She shifted her shoulder trying to remove the hand, but it wouldn't budge. She opened her mouth, lunged forwards, and closed it around the skin of the Šéf's hand, biting down hard! The Šéf screamed out in pain and the hand removed itself, giving Leira a chance to admire her mouth-work, but that wasn't going to stop its owner.

With his unbitten hand he tried to twist her around to face him, tugging on the straps of her dress. She twisted the other way, towards the door on the other side. The chord of her music player tangled up around her arm, snapping it off her ear and taking a chunk of her skin with it. Leira screamed in pain and clutched her ear. The Šéf took the opportunity to grab her arm and yank her back towards him. She pulled her head back, trying to be as far away from him as possible.

The Šéf decided that enough was enough and covered her face with a dark cloth, the last thing she saw was his stupid disgusting grin. He pressed down on her face harder. She couldn't scream, she couldn't see, and she couldn't breathe. She had lost all feeling in her limbs. The only sense she had left was smell, which was now being drowned in dank liquorice. She hated liquorice. She twisted and writhed under the man three times her age, grabbing onto his arm and trying to remove it from her face, but he pressed down harder. The cloth leached and absorbed all of Leira's energy.

The blackness that covered her eyes slowly turned to a deep blue. Wavy lines of water currents flew by her vision, the gleam of sunlight on the surface barely visible in the distance. It was falling away from her. No…she was falling away from *it*. No. She wasn't falling. She was drowning.

Drowning…drowning…drowning…

#

Leira's eyes snapped open, still overwhelmed with panic. She looked around to discern her surroundings, making sure her last memories weren't just some terrible nightmare. The inside of the Šéf's carriage confirmed it. She quickly looked around for him, but he wasn't there, she was alone. She looked down and saw the tangled mess of wires and broken cogs between her legs falling down to the floor; her only set, broken. Her blue dress was frazzled and torn in places from the struggle. She was never going to be able to afford new clothes.

Thoughts raced through her head: *Why has this happened to me? Where did I go wrong? Was this all my fault? Why was this my fault?* And worst of all, the one she hated herself for thinking, *should she be grateful?*

She was smart though, of course it wasn't her fault. The moment she'd been born she'd been destined for this as it had been the case for all colour-haired girls before her. She was bitten by the irony of how putting prices on people's heads made them feel worthless.

She untangled herself and clung on to the remains of her earpiece, making her way over to the tinted window to look outside. The Šéf's precaution became her advantage. Right outside the window was a Blue Guard, standing just a few inches away from her, facing away. Her reflexes told her to duck down, but she quickly realised it wouldn't be able to see her.

Leira peered around, analysing her immediate surroundings. The rusted scrap slabs pieced together like a jigsaw made up the 10ft high city walls. Several people snaked into short queues leading up to the base of the wall, where the Blue Guard searched rigorously through every bag and vehicle entrants wished to bring in with them. There weren't many people wanting to get in, but most were turned away or thrown into holding cells. Only when the Blue Guard's palms were greased with Honeywax did they seem to let anyone in.

Right at the base of the wall, the Šéf had skipped to the front of the queue and was chatting up a Blue Guard, no doubt bribing them to let him in. Or perhaps he was just explaining who he was to them, he did control them after all.

Time to make a move, Leira thought. She slowly shifted herself towards the other side of the carriage, being careful not to alert the Blue Guard standing just outside the window. Her finger pressed a button to the side of the door which caused it to slide open, luckily, silently. She stared at the finger that had pressed the button, freaked out by the idea that it had touched something that the Šéf had no doubt touched moments ago. *What else had that finger touched?* She wiped it on the leather seat of the carriage. It didn't help. Everything she touched felt disgusting and even more *wrong* than usual.

She stepped out from the carriage, onto the ground, ducking behind it. It felt wrong.

She leaned out slightly to the side, to check no one was watching. It felt wrong.

She looked behind her, some roads off to the side, but in the other direction was the vast emptiness of the desert. Right now, that was the most appealing option; she'd heard rumours of towns in the desert where people could seek refuge if they had nowhere else.

Making sure that no one was watching her, she sprinted off into the vast golden ocean.

#

Holliday's heart raced as he realised that he couldn't see the sheriff lying on the operating table. As he fully entered his surgery, he calmed down as he noticed her in the corner, sitting on the chair. He was, however, surprised to see her arms around the shoulders of someone else.

The girl was crying. Not the sort of crying that you do for attention, but the sort where you just can't stop. The sort where something so unbelievably terrible has happened to you, that your brain and body don't quite know how to deal with it, other than by releasing a stream of tears down your face and ruining whatever unlucky surface has found itself beneath your feet. Holliday would worry about his rough metal floor another time. The girl shook Eliza's arm off from around her shoulder and the older woman backed away.

Eliza and Holliday shared a glance, they'd seen people like this enough times now that they could guess what had happened to the girl. There were loads of reasons people ran away, but ultimately, they boiled down to similar things. After all, everyone in Runaway was a runaway.

Holliday quickly relieved himself of his weapon and fetched the girl a glass of water from the tap, placing it down on the cabinet next to her chair. She stared at it. *Smart girl.* Holliday didn't blame her for not trusting the water. It was likely that she'd had her faith in someone broken. *Why else did anyone become a runaway?* For all he knew, it was a glass of water that had caused it. He poured half of it into a separate glass and drank it himself, indicating that it was okay. He knew she needed to drink. The 6-mile run through the desert from the city wasn't easy, but the girl was clearly too busy crying to realise how tired she was.

'Ain't nobody that's not welcome here in Runaway, child,' Eliza told Leira, who was still struggling to work up the courage to allow the sound of her name to come out of her mouth, but from what Holliday could tell from her attempts at mumbling it, it began with an 'L'.

'There's folks like you turning up all the time. Everyone comes here to run away from the Blue Guard. You know, I was the first one here and I was running away from the Šéf too! Not your Šéf of course, the Šéf before.' Holliday recognised the tone in her voice.

She was going for quirky and reassuring, trying to show the girl she understood.

'Do you know how the Šéf came to control the Blue Guard?' she asked. The girl nodded. 'It's all a lie. Everything they tell you.' The girl's eyes widened. So did Holliday's. He'd believed the stories too, that generations ago, at the end of the ancient war, the committee had asked a single brave hero to step forward to lead the final charge. The title, as well as the courage, guile and cunning of a commander, had been passed down through the generations.

'Now, do you really think that someone brave enough to lead a final charge would sink as low as to kidnap someone as important as you? Do you think that anyone who enjoys that much power deserves it?' The girl shook her head after a moment of thought. 'Regardless of what happened all those years ago, and quite frankly I don't believe a word of it, he is not the man they would have you believe. There's someone far more courageous sitting right here in front of me. Here in Runaway, we don't tolerate no one who thinks they're better than anybody else. That's why none of us ever wanna go back.'

The girl visibly suppressed a smile. 'My name is Leira,' she muttered and the Sheriff beamed in response.

'Blue, huh Leira?' the sheriff said, eyeing up the girl's distinctive hair. Leira looked at her, her sniffles momentarily stopping. The sheriff walked over to the tap and stuck her head underneath it so that water poured down her hair. She ran her hands along it, making sure every strand was thoroughly washed, gradually revealing her true colours. Her hair glowed a fantastic bright yellow. She wrung out the water and stood up straight again. 'Comes in mighty handy in the desert, 'specially with bandits around! You lil' lady'd make a mighty fine mermaid!'

Leira didn't really know what the sheriff meant, but nevertheless, she turned to the water, picked up the glass, and drank it eagerly. Colour returned to her face instantly; she'd not realised how thirsty she'd been. Holliday looked at the sheriff, his best friend for the best part of a decade. Even he didn't know she had that hair.

'Enough!' she commanded him, snapping him out of his trance before turning back to Leira. She stared at the floor. 'Been a long while since I saw another girl with colour in her hair. Nearly 50 years. Now, in all my time living in and running this here town, I ain't never shown folks my true hair colour, what it meant and how it got me here out of shame. But, I promise that I will never let it shame me again. More, I will be proud of my yellow and show it off to everyone here. I will do this just for you because we *are* more valuable than everyone else. Not a money value, a life value, more than any amount of Honeywax. I will do this for you, but only on the condition that you accompany me and my friend here on a tour of my little town, and, for a bite to eat at the tavern across the road, because, I don't know 'bout you, but I sure am starving as hell!'

Leira looked at the old sheriff, eyes wise and a smile kind. Holliday looked into her big sad eyes. She was a runaway now, whether she liked it or not.

Four – A Bath in Suspicious Vibrations

W ith a flash, Vale took a picture of the two women who had just spent four Honeywax on a skewer of chocolate-coated rum-buns. She looked at their snack and instantly felt hungry. She hadn't eaten all morning.

It was around lunchtime. The seahawks tweeted and the sun shone brightly down onto the Beirasmus market. Warm snow settled on the tops of the stalls, never quite making it down to the wooden floor of the pier. There were rumours that in some part of the world, snow only fell when it was cold, but Vale didn't believe that; not until she got to see it for herself, at least.

The market was a great place to take pictures of people. Vale had set up her camera in her usual spot, a cramped corner in between a man who sold hand-carved wooden trinkets of fishing boats, and the rum-bun stand. She didn't know why she tortured herself all the time by setting up right next to that tempting smell.

The two women covered themselves and walked off, not wanting their faces made public. Vale had found that a growing problem. She could understand it, but it didn't make her job any easier. She'd been taking pictures of people for an idea for a column she'd had. It was just an idea, so she wasn't being paid for it. She had lots of ideas.

Vale spent most of the day taking pictures, printing off bad quality draft versions and throwing away the ones she didn't like. When she wasn't taking pictures, she was moving her camera out of the way to allow the market-goers to get by. She'd lost count of how many times she'd said 'sorry' and 'Jolly Beirasmus' in the last hour alone. During Beirasmus season, the market was more popular than usual; everyone had come to do their last-minute shopping. Even if Vale celebrated Beirasmus, she wouldn't have anyone to shop for. For the last few years, since she'd stopped talking to Mattai Morieux, she'd not had anyone to buy presents for. Even now, she found it hard to stop herself from buying things she knew he might like. With neither of them having anyone else to celebrate with, they'd have Beirasmus breakfast together and open each other's presents. It was a bittersweet memory. She couldn't comprehend how the man who'd bought her half of the very clothes she was wearing had turned into the man he was now.

By the evening, Vale was hot and sweaty. She'd been in a tight crowd for hours and hours and craved some space. She packed up her camera and slowly forced her way through the marketeers, occasionally stopping to admire the intricate wares at some of the stalls, such as sour babarak or a carved metal bovine figurine. Suddenly, she had another idea. She could open up a stall at the market and sell prints of her photographs! That was certainly one to look into when she got home later that evening, or never.

Finally, she reached the end of the pier and breathed a sigh of relief and tiredness. She placed her camera bag beside her and rested atop the grey stone wall that separated the landmass from the ocean. She looked through her draft printouts from the day and mostly saw people going about their lives. Same old people, same old day. She was sure she even recognised some of them from her own previous photographs. Was her life now so repetitive that she was even taking pictures of the same people doing the same thing? She sighed, letting her same old hands drop to her same old side, staring off into the same old crowd.

Just as she was about to take the same walk home again, she had another one of her brilliant ideas. In actual fact, it was the same idea she'd had before, only then it was tomorrow Vale's problem. Today, Vale decided to make yesterday's tomorrow Vale's problem, today Vale's problem. She jumped down from the wall and walked along the cobbled promenade, scanning the harbour for ships. *Someone here must need a journalist, or a photographer, or ideally, both.*

The first was a small fishing boat. Deserted. *The Rusty Shark* was stacked with crates of dead sea life and was so dejected that it looked like it couldn't even leave the harbour without getting distracted by the bottom of the ocean. Probably not the best option for someone looking to travel to exotic places.

The second was a larger schooner, gently rocking back and forth as the waves underneath crashed against the concrete wall, causing the drone of a bell to softly ring out. A plaque on the side named it the *Salty Sparrow*.

'Alright, m'loverrr?' came a voice from up high. Vale looked up and saw three men sitting, balanced atop a horizontal wooden mast in the rigging. Smoke billowed from each of their mouths as they passed a clockwork cigar between each other. 'Ya lost?' said another.

Two of the three men had beards and their clothing was as rugged as their ship, even more rugged than Vale's. She imagined they were pirates. *That could be exciting, or dangerous, or both*, she thought. She'd applied for enough jobs to know the best way of getting people on her side.

'You boys mind if I take some pictures?' she asked, gesturing to her camera. Asking people for something whilst giving them a compliment—People 101. They shrugged. Vale took out her camera and started taking pictures of the men as they flexed for the camera. Occasionally, she asked a question about the ship to which the answers she got seemed either long and in-depth or short and vague, seemingly at random. They knew a lot about sailing, but little about their own ship, almost as if it wasn't theirs. Vale was sensible enough to realise that the ship was probably stolen. Not wishing to bathe in the suspicious vibrations she was amassing from the pirates any longer, she thanked them for their time, packed away her camera, and continued down the harbour.

A large green tarpaulin protected the largest ship in the harbour from the warm snow. Its masts and sails were about 50ft tall and its dark planks stretched 300ft out from the bowsprit to the taffrail. It was a very large tarpaulin. Wooden beams of scaffolding stretched across the starboard bow and down into the ocean. Vale imagined this thing would definitely be breaking records when it was complete. To be aboard this ship would be a dream come true.

Vale looked around it, searching for signs of life on board.

'Hello?' she hesitated. *An owner? A captain?* There was no one there at all. She peered down over the edge, the wooden hull disappearing beneath the slow waves of the ocean into darkness.

Splash!

Vale suddenly found her face, hair and clothes drenched in ocean water. Her long, soaking hair clung to her face, obscuring her vision of a large black object rising up from the waves. *An octopus?* She scraped her hair off her forehead and flicked her hands, flinging the liquid onto the cobbled ground. It was a good thing her camera was safely packed away, or it surely wouldn't work anymore.

As the black object continued to rise out of the water, Vale's vision cleared, enabling her to see that it was not an octopus at all. It was a machine. It had big, darkened windows on the front, and, what she had thought were limbs were in fact mechanical arms.

Vale had heard about these submersibles but never seen one before. They were usually used for fishing, but the owner of this one had replaced the hooks with Bell-tech® hammers, Diaphragm & Sons™ saws and drills, and Arson Incorporated® welding torches. How they were supposed to work underwater, she had no idea. One by one, the welding torches powered down and the saws stopped spinning.

The submersible stopped on the surface and a hatch on the top slid open.

'Sorry! Sorry! Sorry!' came the apology from the hand that popped out. Vale assumed it belonged to someone. She stood there, slightly shivering and staring at the rest of the stranger as she emerged. 'Sorry! Sorry!' By now the figure had managed to balance herself on top of the submersible as it slowly rocked back and forth. She perfectly adjusted her weight to stay up straight with every rock. She wore a long green lab coat, navy-blue trousers and a pair of welding goggles. Her chin-length hair was let down against her ears. 'So sorry!' she shouted down at Vale, who was incredibly confused. The strange woman stood with her hands on her hips but scratched her ear nervously from time to time. As a trained journalist, Vale was usually good at telling if someone was in charge, but here, her years of lectures, seminars and experience were really letting her down.

'Been meaning to put in some kind of warning signal. Some flashing lights, a loudspeaker or a big flare-gun maybe. Never quite got round to it,' she explained from the top of the black sphere.

'H-h-how would a flare-gun work underwater?' asked Vale, shivering. The woman just frowned down at her.

'Because of the vinegar,' came the answer. Vale was unable to tell if she was joking. She certainly didn't *look* like she was joking. There was no way vinegar could make a flare-gun work underwater, right? *Right!?*

'But, how...' she started before the figure leapt from the top of the submersible towards Vale, and landed expertly next to her on solid ground, only just missing the wall on the way. She was stunned, confused, and amazed, but not necessarily in that order.

'Rocket! Nice to meet you,' said the woman, holding out a hand. Vale was reluctant to take it, given her hand was still soaking wet, but Rocket used her other hand to place Vale's inside hers, shaking it with earnest vigour. Rocket dried her hand on her coat as if it were nothing. Not her own hand, but Vale's. Vale stared at it after Rocket finally let her go.

'That's an odd name,' said Vale, before her face dropped, realising what she was about to introduce herself as. 'I'm Vale.'

'That's nice,' said Rocket. There was a moment of silence as Vale struggled to regain her professionalism. 'Can I help you?' asked the inventor, squinting her eyes at the rugged journalist as if analysing the absurdity of the situation, making sure it was sufficiently absurd for her.

'Erm... yes. I'm a freelance photographer and journalist,' said Vale, tapping her camera bag. 'I was wondering if I might be able to cover the story of this ship you're building. Perhaps I could apply for a job on board as one of the crew? Could get you a lot of publicity to have someone writing up the story and taking pictures. There's clearly a big journey or expedition you're going on here. Am I right? Can I come along?' she asked, detecting perhaps some over-eagerness in her own voice and making a mental note to tone it down for the next sentence.

Rocket frowned at her. Was she disappointed that she'd figured out what she was doing and what the plan was, or something else? Vale just could not figure this woman out.

'Hmm...' Rocket teased.

'I have experience with *City, The Curious*,' said Vale.

'Hmm…' Rocket teased again, drawing out her deliberation in a higher pitch than before. Vale didn't know if the reference would help her. Rocket didn't seem like the kind of person that would read a resume, but it was still worth a try. Rocket stepped back, looking at Vale's entire body, studying her. She was suddenly aware of her rugged clothes, leather cap and red waistcoat; perhaps she should have torn her trousers to try and get the pity hire. She rushed forward, standing right in front of Vale, and looked directly into her eyes. They darted left and right, up and down. She looked around to the side, pulled back Vale's ear and looked behind it as if it would somehow affect her decision. Vale was slightly concerned but couldn't help liking this quirky, mad woman.

'Yes!' said Rocket. Vale's face lit up with delight.

'You are right, we are going on the journey of a lifetime! A journey around the world, and I am the captain!' said Rocket, proud and teasing all at the same time. Vale knew she'd just been played with, and the look on Rocket's face seemed to confirm it.

'But I'm afraid I can't help. You need to talk to the man who is funding the journey. He is covering all the boring administration and paperwork. Just try getting me to write things down and do sums! Ha! Boooring!' Rocket reached into the pocket of her dark green lab coat and pulled out a piece of pink paper and a pencil. She scribbled some notes on it, tore off the segment with writing on and handed it to her. 'Tell him I sent you, he'll recognise my handwriting.'

Vale looked down at the scrap paper. It was the worst handwriting she'd ever seen. She could barely make out the words. As she tried to read the note, she'd failed to notice Rocket's agility as she'd leapt back some four feet to her submersible. From there, she stared down at the photographer.

'When will the ship be ready?' asked Vale. She instantly regretted asking. She got what she wanted; she didn't need to press for more information. But she *was* the press and pressing was what she did.

'Not for a while, I'm working on my own secret experiment.' She placed a finger to her lips, imploring Vale to keep the secret even though she didn't know what it was. She *really* was starting to like the endearing personality of this inventor, this captain. Perhaps her future captain.

Rocket removed her finger from her lips and gave Vale a wink.

'See ya later!' she said before kicking open the hatch and jumping down inside. The humming of its combustion engines gently came to life, and the large black object, which Vale had thought was an octopus, slowly descended down into the dark water.

Vale stood for a moment, watching the water calm. The sun was setting over the ocean, and the warm snow was slowly drying out her clothes. Her heart raced as she thought back over the conversation she had just had with Rocket. She kicked herself for not writing it down like she'd write down a normal interview. *Journey of a lifetime.*

But it wasn't a secure job, yet. She had a meeting with someone. Certainly, this seemed like a great opportunity, and she'd have to try her hardest to convince... *Galileo* to let her come along. The paper was proof that the exchange had happened. It was so fast, it felt like a dream. But no, there the paper was. Rocket's terrible handwriting, in Vale's hand.

She looked up at the giant ship and wondered if it had a name. It was utterly incredible, even covered by a layer of green tarpaulin and a layer of snow. She imagined where it would go. All the strange, strange places. All the strange, strange people. Forget the rum-buns, now she was hungry for adventure.

Her mind returned to Mattai Morieux and his articles on architecture. If she landed this gig, it would knock his out of the park. She was already imagining his face as she disembarked from the ship upon its return, everyone having read her articles. After all that he'd put her through, she was even more determined to get this job now.

She stood herself up straight, her way of focusing her mind. Vale had work to do.

#

Galileo hated when any of his senses were suppressed, but sight was the worst. It reminded him of being trapped in the lockers or being thrown in the bin by his bullies at school. He liked being able to control things, as it made him feel safe. But when he couldn't even control his own vision or movement, that was terrifying. He should never have agreed to let Rocket tie her apron around his face to keep the reveal of the ship to him a surprise. But she'd insisted, and, well, as much as he didn't like surprises, he did appreciate the theatrics she was going for.

Her hands guided him as he struggled across the uneven cobbled promenade. He was all too aware that they were walking next to the ocean, and he didn't entirely trust Rocket not to lead him directly into the water. The sound of the waves splashing up against the sandstone sea wall came worryingly closer.

Other than that, it was silent and deserted, even devoid of the usual smell of baking rum-buns. Touch was Galileo's only remaining sense, and even that was being overwhelmed by the biting warmth of the crisp morning air.

Eventually, Rocket stood him still, and tilted his head slightly to the left. Slowly the apron fell away from his face, forcing Galileo to squint to adjust his eyes to the brightness.

'Ta-da!' said Rocket, who stood in front of him, gesturing behind her with both arms. Galileo took a moment to analyse the photons that were making their way into his vision. He'd expected to see his ship, the Leisurely Ländler, just as beautiful and majestic as he'd painted it in his original designs. He was horrified as he realised Rocket had disobeyed his one condition. The green of the tarpaulin burned. He tried his best to look at it, but it was just too uncomfortable. He focused on the scaffolding on the starboard bow.

'It's not finished?' he asked, accidentally echoing her earlier sentiment when he'd first proposed the project in the workshop.

'Well it's a work in progress. I thought it would go well with all your graphs and charts!' she replied as Galileo bit his lip, trying not to be offended, despite knowing it was a joke. 'There's still a bit of tinkering left to do. What do you think?'

'It would help if I could see it. Did you really have to use green for the cover? I did explicitly say not to use green.'

It was no good, he had to look away. Thankfully, Rocket wandered off towards the ship and ushered him to follow. Perhaps if they went under it, he wouldn't be able to tell the colour.

Annoyingly, Rocket had welded lanterns to the top of the inside of the tarpaulin, bathing Galileo in a sickly green as he walked inside. He kept his head down towards the brown of the deck as Rocket gave him the tour, too busy focusing on ignoring the colour to listen to what she was saying. After she'd shown him around the quarterdeck and looked at the helm, she took him below deck. Finally, Galileo could relax and appreciate his ship. For now, the rooms were bare, Galileo having instructed Rocket to leave the interior design to him. Everything seemed... good.

Rather worryingly, he couldn't spot anything wrong with it, which served only to make him more anxious. *Something* had to be wrong. He scanned over the designs in his photographic memory, but… nothing seemed out of place. The rooms were the right dimensions and the hull had been the right shape. Rocket seemed to have followed his plan down to every last detail. This was a new feeling, was he really beginning to *trust* someone? Rocket of all people? Weeks of stressful letter-writing, filling out forms and organising meetings with people were starting to look like they might actually pay off. He started to imagine the faces of those who had taunted him back at the guild as he stood on his platform, proudly announcing his ship to the people of the city.

Back on the safety of land, and, making sure he was facing *away* from the Leisurely Ländler this time, Galileo had the feeling that his plan might actually work. He couldn't help but smile at Rocket and congratulate her profusely.

He imagined the exact position where his platform might be and where he would be standing to make the announcement. He'd need speakers and a microphone, advertising, journalists; there was so much still to do!

Just as he was about to leave Rocket to it, she called him back and patted over her entire body up and down, looking for something hidden in a pocket. She snapped her fingers in the air as if remembering she didn't have anything at all.

'Ah, nearly forgot. A journalist came by earlier asking about joining up with us. I told her to meet you at the guild for lunch tomorrow,' she said, the smile on Galileo's face transforming itself into a frown. 'Hope that's okay, didn't really know what else to do.'

To Galileo, this was yet another thing to dread and prepare for. He was always the most nervous person in an interview, regardless of which side of the table he happened to be sitting on.

'Fine,' he said, with a sigh.

As he departed, the worry kicked in again. So much was depending on him now, what if he *couldn't* pull this off? His list of things he had to do before they set sail was growing out of hand. For every item he checked off, two more were added. He roughly scratched the back of his head, his way of trying to cope with the stress. Galileo had work to do.

Five – The End of a Movement

Waves of dreams passed over Leira as she slept. Blues, greens, and brilliant yellows swirled around her imaginary night vision like undercurrents swooping beneath the surface of a mountain stream, the light of the rocks underneath reflecting and refracting in a spectacular kaleidoscope. The brilliant yellow intensified, brighter and brighter, obscuring and drowning out all other colour, until it was so bright...

Clunk!

Leira rubbed her bruised head as she ducked below the auto-doc she had just crashed into. She attempted to replay what had happened in her mind.

She was in ~~the City~~ Runaway. She'd fallen asleep ~~in her bed~~ on Doc Holliday's operating table. She'd been there ~~her entire life~~ a week.

The bright light of the desert sunrise shone in through the window, her eyes taking a moment to adjust. The setting of the surgery was becoming somewhat more familiar to her. Even though Leira could easily have her own room in the saloon, Sheriff Eliza refused to let her stay there, insisting that Holliday looked after her instead. Leira didn't complain. She didn't want to be left on her own. Come to think of it, she didn't really want company either. Besides, even the operating table was comfier than the bed she'd had in the city back home.

Home. Where her parents were. Would she ever see them again? Was she completely alone forever? Who could she call family?

Staying in Runaway didn't feel right. She liked Charlie the barmaid, but only because she kept bronze-fish. She loved watching the bronze-fish dance around in their little glass water-cage. *How peaceful that life must be.* She wished she was a bronze-fish.

She liked the pianist as well. He played the tack piano in the corner of the bar and sang songs, mostly about Runaway and the stories that people had to tell. It was the closest thing she had to music now that her earpiece was broken. She still kept it with her, in the hopes that one day it might be repaired. It was everything she owned, a remnant of her past but a clue to her future: a broken earpiece.

She hadn't seen much of Eliza since the first day she'd wound up in Runaway, she did have the entire town to look after, after all. Holliday on the other hand, had been like a surrogate father to Leira and a better one than her real father had ever been. He'd paid for all her food and drink, had taught her to fire a revolver and how to ride a mechanical horse. She was a quick learner. She had tried with all her might not to trust him, but it was difficult. He couldn't do much for the mental scarring of her recent trauma, but he had treated her broken ear the day after she'd arrived, and it was nearly healed now.

In her other spare time, she'd mostly stare out into the vast expanse of the desert, sometimes towards the city, if she was brave. Most of the time though, she didn't feel like doing anything at all.

Eliza and Holliday had asked her to attend a meeting in the saloon, and apparently it was urgent. She rolled herself to the edge of the table and gently climbed down. She went over to the window and closed the blinds, keeping the sun out and making sure no one was looking in when she changed into her blue dress—the only item of clothing she owned, from the borrowed clothes of Eliza's.

As she made her way out of the surgery and across Runway to the saloon, she wondered what their meeting might be about. She wondered if they were going to ask her to do some work for the town. That would be okay, she'd been living off Holliday's money and felt guilty about it, perhaps starting to feel a sense of citizenship for the first time in her life.

Holliday and Eliza were already sitting at a table, drinking ginger crush and sharing a plate of rum-buns, serenaded by silence;

it was too early for the music. They saw Charlie take a break from drying out mugs with a cloth to wave to the girl who had just entered through the automatic metal saloon doors. They glanced towards Leira as she made her way over to them and sat on the chair that was waiting for her. She didn't wave back at Charlie; social interaction made her nervous.

Holliday and Eliza looked at each other, then at Leira.

'Mornin' hun, how are you settling in?' asked the sheriff. She'd kept her word, the light of the tavern reflecting off the bright yellow streak in her hair.

'Fine,' replied Leira. She wasn't.

'Do you have everything you need?' asked Holliday. 'I'm heading to the city later so I could buy anything you need for someone to collect'. Eliza discretely nudged Holliday with her elbow. He looked at her in reflexive anger, rubbing his ribs.

'Yes,' replied Leira. She didn't.

'Have you met everyone here, they're all being nice and friendly?' asked Eliza.

'Yes,' replied Leira. She almost wished they weren't, just so she could get the perfect trifecta of lies. 'What's this about?'

Eliza paused, and turned to Charlie, who was filling up a barrel with drinkables and asked her for some water for the table. Water was Leira's favourite drink.

'The doc here briefly mentioned, he's out of town for...'

'For the foreseeable future,' Holliday finished her sentence. 'I got a place on a ship to search for ingredients for... uh... medicine and stuff.'

No, Leira thought to herself. *This was not happening, again.*
She already felt a twitch of abandonment sear through her heart.
Holliday was sitting right there but suddenly she felt like he was a
million miles away. Her brain refused to accept it. Her body froze.
Charlie placed a glass of water in front of her and she tipped it
down her throat like a whale swallowing plankton.

Whilst she had been busy panicking internally, Holliday and
Eliza had continued talking. Presumably, they were talking about
what the arrangement would be, where she would stay, how she
would live. Leira didn't hear a word of it. Or maybe she did, she
just didn't *want* to hear a word of it.

'Ya got all that, hun?' concluded the sheriff.

'Yes,' replied Leira. She hadn't. They looked down at her,
doubtfully. She quickly wiped away a tear in the hopes that they
hadn't spotted it roll down her face.

Holliday lifted up his silver fob-watch and opened it. He made
some comment about the time, which Leira ignored, before
standing up from his chair and taking his leave. Eliza concurred,
she had work to do, as always. Leira didn't move, she was frozen
to the chair, simply watching as her two adoptive parents left the
tavern. Charlie wandered over and took up a seat opposite her,
Leira's eyes following her down like the eyes of a star-squid clung
to the side of a fish tank. She silently poured more water into
Leira's empty glass.

'I overheard...' she began, before being cut off by the sound of
the chair legs scraping against the matt floor and removing some of
the red paintwork in the process. Before Charlie could react, Leira

was on her way to the automatic saloon doors, having leapt up so violently the freshly poured drink now formed a shallow tablecloth. She sidestepped through the automatic metal doors which were proving too slow for her and left Charlie alone in her saloon with slightly damp elbows.

#

Waves of nightmares passed over Leira as she tossed and turned. Reds, purples and dull dark blacks stormed around her imaginary night vision like waves crashing against the face of a cliff, the water moving back and forth in a dizzying flurry. The dull dark black darkened, blotting out the only patches of colour. All light was dying, she was falling deeper below the surface...

Clunk!

Leira instinctively rubbed her head, but this time it was her back that hurt, and she quickly relocated her hands to rub there instead. She looked up to see the underside of Doc Holliday's operating table, and, for the last week and a day, her bed. She noted that she hadn't seen the underside of it before. It wasn't very interesting, but it provided a momentary distraction from the pain in her back.

This was the first night Leira had attempted to sleep alone in a building, or alone anywhere for that matter. It didn't help that this was a somewhat strange building, and two sudden abandonments in the space of a week were hardly the baby steps she'd hoped for.

Holliday had left the evening before, beginning the trek across the desert and towards the city. He'd taken most of his possessions with him. She wondered how long he'd be gone for. Leira imagined him getting further and further away. By dawn, he and his clockwork horse would be at the city gates, and, ironically, near to where she'd last seen her parents and the Šéf. She shuddered at the thought of *him*.

Leira crawled across the cold hard floor towards the window and dragged herself up the wall so she could see out. The desert at night was a symphony of chirping, flautish Krokkits, harsh percussive crosswinds, and howling wild brass Padocs. The moo of a Rural Wood-Bovine occasionally chimed through to signify the start or end of a movement. Most movements were *attacca*[1] (or extremely subtle when not).

All she saw were the few lights that remained on in Runaway, likely the town hall at the end, and the tavern. The town hall light always remained on and Charlie always stayed late to clean up in the tavern. Two smaller lights caught Leira's eyes. Off on the horizon, in the direction of the city... could be Holliday. Two became three. Three became... five... eight... twelve...

Leira's heart skipped a beat as she realised that they were getting closer. She ran over to the cabinet and opened every drawer. In the fourth one she opened, she found Holliday's monocular, the one thing that Holliday had forgotten. Leira definitely hadn't stolen it from him so she could look at the stars. Syranei was her favourite constellation. Pressing it to her left eye she looked in the direction of the light.

Some figures were definitely on horseback, but it was still difficult to see. She held the monocular with her left hand only and

---

[1] Attacca – Musical term signifying the fusion of movements in a work with no break. The audience must strive to hold in their raucous coughing until the end of the piece.

used her right to twist the dial on the side, zooming in and focusing it on the figures.

She recoiled in horror, recognising the distinctive pristine flags and uniform of the Blue Guard. Twenty in total, swarming on the town of Runaway in perfect formation. Leading them, the Šéf. One week. It had been just enough time for the Šéf to prepare a hunting party and a plan. They were looking for Leira. She reckoned they'd be there in under five minutes.

Her entire body wanted her to freeze on the spot, but adrenaline kicked in. She gathered her broken earpiece, some Honeywax, and, still clutching onto the monocular, sprinted out of the surgery and over Runway to the tavern. Catching her dress on the slow automatic saloon doors, Leira struggled inside.

'Morning, partner,' said Charlie, who was sticking up bottles of ginger crush on the rack behind her. She turned her head and looked confused. Clearly, she wasn't used to company in the tavern at this ungodly hour. Leira said nothing, placing her bag down in front of the bar and jumping up to lean over the top of it. She scanned behind it looking for any food and drink, grabbing the only bottle of ginger crush left out.

'Err, the sheriff's working in the town hall, if it's her you're looking for?' queried a confused bartender. 'I'm sure she'd be happy to see you.'

Leira ignored her, instead grabbing a sandwich from the cooler on top of the counter. She replaced it with Holliday's Honeywax as payment.

'Leira?'

Again, she ignored her, still running on adrenaline. Leira went to the window and spied out with the monocular. The storm of Blue Guard was just two minutes away and closing in quick. By the time she'd put down her monocular, Charlie was looking out beside her.

'Warn Eliza. I'll distract them. Capisce?' she said. Leira nodded. With one hand on her shoulder, Charlie guided the terrified girl to the back door of the saloon, grabbed a revolver from under the bar and pressed it into her hand. 'Be careful.'

She pushed her out the door quickly, hoping to god she'd be okay as she watched the girl creep behind the back of the buildings up towards the clock tower at the top of Runway. She returned to the bar and grabbed a glass, smashing it on the table as hard as she could.

She listened carefully to the conversation outside between the Šéf and his Blue Guard.

'You two, check it out. Kill anyone that isn't the girl. The rest of you, search the town,' instructed the Šéf. Without needing to be told twice, two of the Blue Guard climbed down from their horses and made for the saloon whilst the others proceeded to kick down every door to every building.

Hidden behind the bar, Charlie had grabbed a rifle and was prepared. She leaned over the top and quickly fired towards the entrance. The first of the Blue Guard fell to the ground, dead. The other quickly ran in as she was reloading, stepped over its comrade's body and flipped over a table for cover.

The Blue Guard waited patiently behind the table for Charlie to pop up again, which she did a moment later. Expecting to find another guard there, she looked around confused, just for a second. It was more than enough time for the Blue Guard to jump up and fire. The shot echoed around the saloon as Charlie staggered backwards into the wall behind the bar, clutching just below her left collarbone, pained surprise on her face. Finally, she fell forward, draped over the bar she was doomed to look after even in death.

#

Leira gave Eliza a fright as she stumbled in through the doors to the town hall. She looked terrified, pathetic even. With a monocular slung around her neck, a revolver in one hand and earpiece in the other hand, Leira looked up at the sheriff, a sad looking mess of a broken girl.

'Ch-Ch-Charlie…' she started in between deep, panicky breaths. 'D-d-dead'

'Hey, take it easy. What's going on?'

Leira gave up talking and pointed to the window. Eliza peered out, the sight of the Blue Guard instilling a burning rage deep inside. She put her hands on Leira's shoulders and turned her so that they were face to face. Tears streamed down the girl's cheeks. Eliza used a hand to wipe them before they reached her mouth.

'We're gonna get outta this, okay?'

Leira nodded.

'Good. Follow me,' she said, dashing to the entrance. They crouched at the door together and Eliza opened it a crack so that they were hidden but had a good view of the street. She pointed to the stables.

'On the count of three, you're gonna run to the barn and you're gonna hide there.' Eliza hated that she was telling the girl to do this. Her look said *I can't* but she knew she had to. She knew how capable she was. 'Get you a horse and get out of Runaway.'

Leira shook her head vigorously.

'Please, you have to. Head for the city. Find the doc. Don't stop for nuthin', ya hear?' she instructed regretfully. 'Tell him I'm sorry... it was worth a shot.'

Eliza ran her hands through the girl's hair, moving her closer so that she could kiss her forehead.

'Three... two...'

Leira dashed. Eliza winced and held her breath, keeping one eye on the girl and one on the guards further down. Time seemed to lapse in slow motion as she ran. As she opened the barn door, Eliza breathed again. Thankful that Leira was safe, at least for the next few minutes, she tipped the brim of her Stetson and stood back up.

They were getting more desperate. What did it mean for the city, that the Šéf would attack Runaway for one colour-haired girl? He played for high stakes, but whatever they were, it wasn't worth Leira's freedom.

Eliza dye-brushed her hair with the tool in her coat pocket to hide her yellow, and made her way outside. She stood in the middle of Runway, facing down to the entrance of the town. She squinted her eyes against the sun, which was starting to rise over the horizon, just about discerning the... six Blue Guard as they lined up in formation in front of her. The Šéf had climbed back onto his high horse, looking down across the town he had no right to believe he was in charge of. Eliza glared at the Šéf as he got closer. It wasn't the one she'd run from, but she recognised him and hated him for what he'd done to Leira just as she'd hated her own Šéf for what he'd done to her.

'Get out of my town,' she demanded. The Šéf looked down at Eliza. The three guards on either side of him aimed their rifles at her. She wasn't afraid of him. She'd faced the Blue Guard before, and won. She knew their secret and what the Šéfs did to them to make them obey orders and to turn them into a force to be reckoned with. She'd almost pity the Blue Guard, if they hadn't chosen to go through the mechanisation process, 'provisioning' as they called it, and if they didn't seem to enjoy their jobs so much. She looked between them all; insufferably identical and deprived of difference.

Eliza looked up at the Šéf. She was alone, her only visible armament a piercing stare. He was perturbed by her.

'Give me the colour-haired girl, and we go quietly,' his booming voice echoed down the corrugated rooftops of Runway. Something was wrong... where were the other guards she'd seen?

'Her name's Leira,' replied Sheriff Eliza calmly. With both hands she spun up two revolvers out of a holster on either side of her, each aimed at 47-degree angles and fired. The Šéf grinned momentarily, realising there was no way she could have hit with that angle, but before he realised what had happened, all six of his Blue Guard fell to the ground dead. Eliza mentally congratulated herself on remembering the exact placement of the buildings and the angles at which they faced Runway, before watching the Šéf's face turn from smug to scared. 'Now git,' she demanded again.

As she looked at the Šéf once more, she saw the scared look on his face dissolve into smugness. He appeared to be looking behind her, slowly Eliza turned around...

Bang!

#

Leira peered through the small crack in the barn door as the Blue Guard rampaged down the street, systematically knocking down doors and searching every inch of every shop and every house. Occasionally she would hear gunfire; they were slaughtering everyone.

She wiped away a single remaining tear before, once again, adrenaline kicked aside any feeling of post-traumatic sickness or imminent survivor's guilt she had. She stored her few belongings into a compartment on the side of the mechanical horse that was tied up at the back of the barn and made sure it was fully secured. With no time to lose, she checked her revolver—9 bullets— unhooked the fuel supply pipe from underneath and jumped aboard.

She flicked a switch on the side of the metal head, just as Holliday had shown her. The horse whinnied and raced off forward, smashing the barn doors wide open. Leira galloped down Runway, wind rushing through her black and blue hair, not bothering to stop to let the three Blue Guard get out of her way. *They deserved to be flattened.* Just a shame the Šéf wasn't one of them. A trail of dust followed Leira out of Runaway as she swerved around Eliza's body.

'Get her!' she heard the Šéf scream at his remaining Blue Guard. It didn't take long before a herd of them were chasing after her through the desert. She prayed that Holliday's lessons were good enough. They were catching up, the machines of the Blue Guard seemed to have more horsepower than hers. A four-foot sand dune lay ahead. Leira braced herself, and yanked on the reins, jumping over it and landing perfectly on the other side. She carefully looked back, noticing the Blue Guard swerving to avoid the dune. She managed to raise the corner of her mouth in a smile, having out-manoeuvred her pursuers.

Another approached on her left. She kept one eye on it and one on the route ahead. It brought itself in line with Leira, and carefully let go of its reins, unhooked one foot from the straps and prepared to leap across to Leira's horse. Leira pulled her own reins with her left hand, forcing the horse to the right as the guard jumped across. The guard fumbled mid-air, managing to grasp one hand onto Leira's foothold. Its lower half bumped and scraped against the ground as they sped through the harsh desert, the rider-less horse abandoning its owner. The guard turned and swivelled, trying to get a better hold. Leira aimed over her shoulder, down at the struggling guard and fired. The first shot served only to take the guard's tall blue hat off. The second, caught the guard's leg. It grunted in pain and relinquished her foothold, tumbling into the hot sand before vanishing in a cloud of dust. Leira thought the reaction was odd, surely a bullet to the leg would hurt more?

71

They weren't going to give her time to think about this, however. A moment later, four more Blue Guard appeared out of the dust, racing towards her. She turned to face ahead and kept her head down as the bullets flew past her. They came in a rhythm of two, the bang of the shot being fired and then a whoosh of the bullet flying by her ears.

She pressed herself down into the horse, leaning forward and moving her hands up the reins, just as Holliday had shown her. The mechanical horse sped up, allowing her to maintain a constant distance between her and the guards. Bullets continued whizzing by. She needed to act quickly. They weren't going to give up easily. All or nothing; Leira against the world. She'd lost everything, and it was about time for her final stand, literally.

She kicked a button by her right foot to put the horse on auto-jockey. She unhooked both feet, carefully turned herself around to face backwards and with all her strength lifted herself upright with her hands outstretched for balance.

Leira aimed her revolver down at the guards chasing her with her right hand and hoped for a miracle. The first shot fell dead into the sand. Leira ducked a shot from below. She fired three more in rapid succession. She staggered, realising she'd hit the front leg of the horse in the middle, toppling both it and the Blue Guard over, a minor victory.

This was hopeless. There were still so many of them and they were relentless. She needed to stop them all, with four remaining bullets, but if she'd learnt anything from Holliday and Eliza, it was that situations like these required outside-the-horse thinking.

Slowly, Leira made her way back down into the riding position, the Blue Guard once again catching up with her. She looked around her mechanical horse as she sped through the sandy plains, looking for something that she could use against them:

Speed gears—maxed out on full, she should probably leave it there.

Luggage compartment—still contained her music player and a packed lunch. That was no good, one had sentimental value and the other she'd need later.

The Blue Guard drew ever closer.

Then she remembered… fuel supply. As quick as she could, she let herself slide down the side of the horse, watching the machinery work its magic on the legs and torso. She reached her hand underneath, holding on to her saddle with the other, felt around, and twisted open the cap. A steady stream of fuel formed a line in the sand, drawing out Leira's path behind her. She waited a few seconds before climbing back up onto the saddle and looking behind her. The Blue Guard were just about to come into line with her fuel deposit…

Nearly there…

She aimed her revolver at the ground and fired a single shot at her fuel supply, sending a firestorm surging along the line, trailing in the sand behind her. It raced towards the Blue Guard and engulfed them in flames. Leira shielded her face as the entire group of guards and their horses exploded causing a shower of shards to fly in every direction, their bodies being flung up into the air. She turned forward again so that her hair could protect her from the heat of the fireball.

For the time being, Leira was safe. She made herself comfortable on the horse and felt proud that she still had three bullets remaining. She slackened her grip a little and sped off through the desert and towards the daunting and rapidly approaching walls of the city.

Six – Oblivious Co-operation

M attai Morieux discreetly read his copy of *City, The Curious*, the only newspaper in the city, the one from which the entire population formed their opinions of the world, of current affairs, and of everything. He was exceedingly proud to be able to call himself a regular columnist in that publication.

He glanced over the top of the newspaper to see his target rise from her table, tuck under her wooden chair and make her way to the bathroom, leaving her companion to read the menu. He wouldn't be where he was today without Vale. She'd called it plagiarism when she found out what he'd done, he'd called it oblivious co-operation.

Mattai had found himself in The Eclipse for his meal, the restaurant adjacent to the Astronomers' Guild. He'd been asked for ID on the way in. He was not a member, of course, but his fake card had sufficiently convinced the woman on the door that he was. Some might have called it fraudulent, but he couldn't help it if his beautiful self-portrait just happened to look like the Astronomers' Guild membership card. He hoped she wouldn't be punished *too* much if she was ever found to have let in a non-member. With all the money he'd made from the newspaper, he was used to restaurants like these. A big tall ceiling was decorated with tapestries and works of art and archways lining the walls. It was split over two levels. The big wooden doors that formed the entrance were on the lower level along with some of the tables. The kitchen and the rest of the tables were on the upper level. The two were connected by a small set of wooden stairs. From his position on the upper level, Mattai faced towards the kitchen with a prime view of where Vale had been sitting.

He watched Vale's companion intently, illuminated by the single flame that flitted in the centre of the table. Some might have called it spying, he called it *veiled* research. The man looked fairly young, wore a long brown frock and had a stressed look about him, as if there was something constantly worrying him. Mattai got the feeling he always had something to do, but what business could a struggling photojournalist have with an astronomer such as him? He presumed he was an astronomer. He was determined to find out. After all, this could potentially lead to more oblivious co-operation.

A waiter in a white tuxedo and a bow tie approached the astronomer's table, addressing him by his name: *Galileo*. Mattai quickly dropped his paper to his table, wrote that down discreetly on his pad and quickly raised the paper back to cover his face should Vale return.

Galileo ordered ginger crush for both himself and Vale, but to Mattai's surprise, he proceeded to order a third. *Was there someone else coming?* He looked over his shoulder towards the big wooden doors on the lower level, but they remained stubbornly shut. He returned his attention to Galileo, who was frantically scribbling something down onto a large sheet that covered most of the table. Sketches? Blueprints? Equations? Mattai couldn't quite make out what it was from his position.

Vale returned to her chair obscuring his vision of Galileo and what he was doing. She drank her entire beverage in two eager gulps before taking the second to last roll of bread from a wicker basket that was holding down some parchment, and demolishing it. It was rare she got to eat this much food in a day let alone for lunch. Mattai figured that Galileo would be paying.

They talked and Mattai listened intently. It was hard to pick up complete sentences with all the background noise of the restaurant and him being several feet away, but from what he could gather, she wanted to be part of his crew. A camera crew perhaps? Maybe he was considering hiring her to take pictures of stars for the astronomy page of *City, The Curious*?

Vale reached down to the side of her chair and inside her large tatty canvas satchel. She produced her camera; the same old vintage one she'd been using ever since he'd first met her. It was cute how she couldn't afford to upgrade and was so attached to that one. She showed it to Galileo who seemed keen to understand her work and the theoretical and physical workings of the camera. Mattai glanced above his paper and scoffed. *He'd be much more impressed by my camera,* Mattai thought to himself as he quickly hid again, realising he may have scoffed a little too loudly. By now, he was convinced that this was a job interview for some kind of astrophotography. There was no way he was going to let this opportunity go to Vale.

Vale packed away her camera and proceeded to take the final roll of bread in the basket, load it with cheese and eat it as if she'd never eaten food before. It would probably be a few moments until interesting conversation happened between them again, what with her mouth mostly full of…

'Crêpe, sir?' asked the waiter, causing Mattai to nearly jump out of his seat. 'It's complimentary.' Mattai declined the appetizer, but took the opportunity to order his main course.

In fact, he'd been so caught up in his ~~spying~~ veiled research, he hadn't even had time to properly study the menu. He panicked, ordering something random from the 'rehydratable' section, but only because he couldn't pronounce the word 'thermostabilizable'. The waiter took his menu and left, by which time Vale had finally finished scoffing bread and cheese. He knew she'd be able to take a whole meal as well, though she was so skinny he wasn't quite sure the biology of that was even possible. No doubt Vale herself would make an interesting case study for an article in the health section of the paper. He wrote that idea down.

Another tuxedo-laden figure approached Galileo and Vale's table. This time, the tuxedo was black and the figure wearing it was carrying a small stringed instrument on her shoulder, clearly intending to serenade what she thought must be a romantic couple out on a dinner date. Well, it was a candle-lit meal in a fancy restaurant, so it was an easy mistake to make. Mattai knew better and Vale was definitely not the dating sort. Although, this man Galileo did look awkward and stressed enough to take up the part. Not that Mattai knew anything about what it was like to date Vale, nobody did, but after years and years of being her best friend, being dragged around museum after museum, he imagined it would be stressful.

The two looked at each other tentatively, neither of them brave enough to reject the girl who seemed so keen to play for them. The two waited patiently for her to stop and take a bow before clapping as she left. Mattai silently giggled to himself at their awkwardness.

Once again, Vale reached into her satchel, this time extracting several dozen prints and spreading them out over the tabletop. The glare from the candlelight prevented Mattai from seeing what they were over the top of his paper, but he guessed they were shots of stars, moons and/or constellations. Either way, it must have been a portfolio of some sort. Galileo was pointing at different pictures, Vale explaining what they were. Occasionally he would stop her to ask her a question about something. There was still a chance for Mattai to jump in afterwards; it seemed like she didn't have the job yet. He recalled passing a library on his way to the restaurant, perhaps he could sneak in and grab some pictures. They'd certainly be of good enough quality to convince this Galileo man to hire him. At the very least, they'd be better than the ones taken from Vale's shoddy equipment.

Suddenly, silence smothered The Eclipse. Everyone was staring at Mattai, including Galileo and Vale. He scrambled to hide himself behind the paper, but it looked unnatural. *Surely* his cover was blown. But he noticed that they were not in fact looking at him. Carefully, he traced several eye-lines down to the level below, so that his face was always hidden by the paper. Everyone was staring at the front door of the restaurant which was now open.

There stood a small figure in a long, white top with golden tassels, a red velvet coat and a pink and blue skirt. As the figure slowly struggled towards the steps, he noticed her legs were attached to strings which flew up into the ceiling. *No, strings from the ceiling controlled her legs!* All eyes in the restaurant followed the marionette as she made her way towards the stairs.

The marionette reached the bottom of the stairs, Mattai was bemused by her. He didn't know what to make of it. Who was she, and what was she doing in the Astronomers' Guild restaurant? He was sure it would make a *very* interesting story.

'Read all about it! Strings and a snack! Local alien gets a taste of home!'

He scrolled through the prospective headlines in his head, always thinking about what would make an audience want to read his articles, but never considering the subject. For him, the story of an alien going to the Astronomers' Guild restaurant to remind her of her home was a winner.

Mattai had been so caught up in mentally exploiting the marionette for his journalistic purposes, that he hadn't noticed both Galileo and Vale jump out of their seats to go and help her up the stairs. He squirmed as they each took one of her arms, taking the weight off the strings. If Vale were to turn around, she would see him, recognise him and surely cause a scene. He knew he should've worn the fake moustache. Covering his face at this point would draw attention. He could only watch and hope that she was too focused on helping her up the stairs to spot him.

The marionette made it up the first step with their help. Vale and Galileo moved each foot simultaneously to help her up the next one.

She made it up the second step just fine too, Vale and Galileo climbing again to be in line with her.

On the final step her strings faltered. A foot caught the edge and she slipped down, finally breaking the eerie silence the restaurant was simmering in. Vale quickly ducked down to catch her before her whole body fell to the floor. She carefully lifted her up and put her back on the step before looking over towards her table and right in Mattai's direction!

Had she seen him?

He breathed a sigh of relief as they guided the marionette back to their table, Galileo letting go to pull out her chair before helping her down as fast as he could. *The third ginger crush, of course! But what on earth could Vale want with an astronomer and a marionette? Curiouser and curiouser.* She and Galileo returned to their seats.

Slowly, the atmosphere in the restaurant returned to normal and Mattai relaxed, safe from Vale's gaze. The marionette was positioned closer to him than the other two, so he was able to hear some of her words more clearly, even though she was clearly very nervous. Her name was Veroushka. She liked tea and cake, looking at the stars and wandering around aimlessly. As their conversation continued, the marionette appeared to relax, her face paint widening with glee as Galileo stopped a waiter so that he could order her tea and cake. She wasn't used to being treated with such respect, so this was a nice change. Being an astronomy café, they only had space cake, but this suited Veroushka just fine.

'Veroushka telegraphed me last week, she has paid to come on the journey,' explained Galileo to Vale as she carefully took the hand of the marionette. Veroushka giggled.

'Enchantée! I'm really not that delicate you know!' she said, shaking Vale's hand back. 'It's just the movement that is slightly difficult.'

'Was it you that I saw at the fairground a few weeks ago?'

'Oui, madame! You were the photographer!' Veroushka explained that she saw loads of people, but the photographer had stood out to her as someone who had looked warm and friendly despite her rugged appearance. Mattai imagined Veroushka was probably the best in the city at not judging on sight. *What an inefficient prude.*

Galileo was clearly surprised that Vale and Veroushka had met before or were at least aware of each other's existence. Their conversation was animated. Vale pressed Veroushka on details about herself, not being rude or exploitative like Mattai would have been, but instead curious and intrigued about a subject which she knew little about, whilst still remaining professional. Mattai doubted anyone other than Vale would have given the marionette the chance to talk, such was the fate of people who were *different*, but such was the compassion of Vale. Veroushka clearly could not stop talking about herself, even when the details of her past started to become vague and blurry. Her audience of two, however, listened patiently and intently at her ramblings. She didn't even stop to pour her tea when it finally arrived.

At the same time, Mattai's meal arrived. The waiter approached his table with a covered silver platter and a steaming hot kettle. He'd been so caught up in trying to listen to their conversation that he hadn't realised how hungry he was. The waiter put down the platter and the kettle and lifted off the lid. Lying within was a yellow and brown assortment of shrivelled vegetables and cheeses at which Mattai simply stared. The waiter left him to his confusion. After tentatively examining and surgically dissecting his meal with his utensils, Mattai decided to go for it, slowly raising a spoonful of food to his mouth, opening, entering, closing, chewing… spitting out onto the plate. He wouldn't be trying that again.

By now, he was sure he'd figured out what was going on. Galileo was an astronomer, building a rocket to send Veroushka back home and he wanted Vale to film it to cover the story. It made total sense and was potentially a good gig, one that would suit Mattai just fine. But if Vale was getting the job, well, he'd just have to do something about it wouldn't he? There had to be some kind of superior to this man Galileo, someone whom he could go to directly to get the job. It was just a question of finding the right person. Perhaps he could even find someone in this very building. He would do anything to stop the job going to that uptight…

'Bit rich, sir?' asked the waiter, gesturing down to the mess on Mattai's plate and causing him to once again nearly jump out of his seat. 'That dish is not to everyone's tastes, particularly not to those with less tuned taste buds.' He shooed off the magical teleporting waiter and continued to listen.

The rest of their conversation provided little insight to help Mattai's veiled research in any way. Veroushka talked about herself, Vale talked about photography and Galileo talked about astronomy, all passionate about their own subject.

Finally, their food arrived with a steaming hot kettle just as Mattai's had. He hadn't known what to do with his kettle, so by now his was surely cold. Mattai watched as Galileo picked out the green-coloured items, and poured the boiling water onto his shrivelled food. *So that's what you were supposed to do.* Mattai poured the contents of his kettle onto the remaining remnants on his plate. To his disgust, the cold water just made them soggy. For Galileo, however, the food transformed into a brilliant platter of colour that made Mattai's mouth water with jealousy! Vale's mouth watered too, instantly grabbing her kettle and coating her food in boiling water, not wasting a single second before shoving entire mouthfuls of roasted urban wood bovine into her mouth. She instantly regretted it as the heat spread throughout her pain receptors and she had to wave a hand in front of her face to try and cool it down. Her attempts were futile, so she ended up having to extract the mess of half-chewed food from her mouth with her hand. It seemed like neither him nor Vale were having any luck at this restaurant. She wiped her greasy hand on a napkin, much to Veroushka's amusement and Galileo's disgust. Veroushka chose to not cover her cake in boiling water. Instead, she carefully guided her fork down to the chocolatey icing, scraped off a piece, and carefully guided it back to her mouth.

After their meal ended, the three shook hands and parted ways, leaving Galileo to pay a rather more expensive Honeywax bill than he was expecting. It was hard to tell, but from his position, Mattai was sure the meeting had gone well for Vale. He would have to be quick if he were to get this job. He looked over to the left to face away from Vale as she walked past his table and down the stairs. After Galileo paid his bill and left the restaurant, he called over a waiter and paid his own. Mattai got up and walked down the stairs to the exit, winked at the woman at the door and left the guild.

Seven – Claustrophobia and Other Conditions

S heriff Eliza always made sure that Runaway was self-sustainable. Like any civilisation, however big or small, times change. People become immune to treatment. Some medicines become outdated and new diseases manifest themselves for which there are no treatments. In the small town of Runaway, Eliza had given the task of keeping everyone alive and healthy to Holliday, so it was up to him to source out new ingredients and create remedies from them. She had given him permission, along with a generous proportion of the town's treasury, to find a ship and travel the world in search of such ingredients, and, after rumours of a new expedition had reached them in Runaway, it had only taken a few letters back and forth with a man called Galileo to get Holliday aboard. He'd tried to source medicines from the city, but the healthcare there was pretty much non-existent. Holliday alone was considered light-years ahead of his time, although only by himself.

As he sat against the leg of his mechanical horse in the queue at the city walls, smoking his early morning cigar, his thoughts turned back to the girl who had unexpectedly turned up in his surgery. He'd been training her up to look after herself in his absence, teaching her how to handle firearms and some simple survival tips, such as how to tell if a plant is poisonous and how to skin animals. She'd come a long way in such a short period of time. Now, he'd left her in the town with the sheriff, for which he felt guilty. She'd obviously formed an attachment to him just as he had to her, but he was leaving for the good of the town. He couldn't forget his responsibility to all the runaways. He was sure she'd be fine.

Eliza had warned him that security would be tighter on the border than it would have been when he first became a runaway. To that end, she'd given him a separate pouch of Honeywax to be used to *persuade* the Blue Guard to let him into the city. As he watched the people at the front get rejected, and the people behind them, and the people behind them, he got more and more nervous.

A Blue Guard gestured for him to move forward, so he put out his cigar with a finger and groggily stood up with a grunt. He walked to the back of his pack horse to check on his suitcases. He had four in total. They were identical and mostly carrying everything he owned, but he'd optimistically left one empty for bringing back his new discoveries. He could have sworn he saw one swaying slightly more than it should have done, but he chalked it up to his imagination. He was thirsty after the long night riding through the desert and desperately wanted a bite to eat. Holliday pressed a button on the head of his horse. It whirred to life and followed his guiding hand which led it to the gate under the 10ft high, patchwork metal wall.

Only a wooden shutter separated Holliday and his horse from the city. A transparent screen separated them from a bored Blue Guard who was sitting inside a small cubed building.

'Documents please,' droned the guard. Holliday could have forgiven anyone for thinking that the Blue Guard were as lifeless as his horse, their monotone voices not entirely unlike his companion's whirring mechanical parts. Eliza had told him their secret, but cold metal parts didn't excuse cold malignant hearts. There was no forgiving their lack of empathy. He did as he was told, placing a dusty roll of parchment in the tray that spanned both his side of the screen and the guard's side. He'd taken the liberty of wrapping up 20 Honeywax inside before setting off. He gulped as he watched the guard unwrap the parchment and look at the persuasion inside. Either this would go well for him, or he could well find himself exploring the world from the inside of a jail cell, or worse.

The guard swiftly pocketed the Honeywax and waved him through without even looking at him, or the documents. *Still human enough to take a bribe then huh?* If this was the extent of their security measures, Holliday sure was glad he didn't live in the city anymore, as money clearly meant more to them than the survival and well-being of the population. He'd already noted the cleanliness of their uniform and the perfect symmetry of their spotless flags. *Vanity must have meant more to these guys than safety.* The wooden shutter creaked and clattered as it opened upwards, folding into the metal wall above. The guard returned Holliday's Honeywax-less parchment and he guided his horse through the gate.

He was in.

#

After hours of riding, Leira had finally caught up. Watching from a distance under the cover of dawn, she weighed up the pros and cons of hiding in the suitcase. She hoped with everything she had there'd be enough room in one of them. If she went up to Holliday directly, there was no way that the Blue Guard wouldn't see her. She'd be arrested and taken straight back to the Šéf. It probably wouldn't end well for Holliday either. At least if she hid in the suitcase there was a chance the Blue Guard wouldn't find her.

Either way, she didn't have much time to decide. Holliday rested against his horse. She dismounted from hers and slowly walked it closer, hiding behind it whenever a guard turned in her direction. He was only a few feet away, so she ran for it, jumping up into the compartment holding Holliday's suitcases. It took her three attempts to find the empty one before she climbed inside and zipped it up around her. The inside of Holliday's case was even less interesting than the underside of his operating table. She could just about see the furred inner lining that was already beginning to itch her skin and infest her nose with the grim burning of dead animal. It was hard not to throw up, but she knew if she did, it would make the rest of her journey even more unbearable.

Her whole body jerked forwards, crashing her head into the side of the case as the horse whirred to life, moving forwards just a few steps before stopping again. She couldn't see anything, but she guessed they were at the guard's booth. This was it, if they searched his cases, she would be found, and everything would be ruined.

She seemed to wait for ages and ages. The feeling of waiting in a carriage breezed over her in a wave of déjà vu; it wasn't helping her feeling of sickness. She breathed more heavily, unconsciously trying to get as much oxygen as possible.

She was trapped in a tiny dark suitcase. It smelled disgusting and the hairs continued to prickle her skin all over making her entire body feel dirty.

She breathed harder, and harder.

Everyone in Runaway was dead. She'd watched as Eliza's body had dropped to the ground and hordes of Blue Guard had broken into the houses and executed the runaways she'd only just learnt to tolerate. Mouth closed, her nose and heart were working overtime in getting oxygen around her body.

They *were* going to find her. They *were* going to kill her. They'd probably also kill Doc Holliday and her parents.

She felt like a knife was stabbing her slowly in the neck and her lungs were going to explode out of her body. Questions she'd long forgotten resurfaced in her mind: *Was this my fault? Do I deserve this? Why was this my fault?*

Once again, the horse suddenly trotted forwards, throwing her body around the case, this time smashing her arm against the back and snapping her mind back out of the panic attack.

Somehow, she'd made it back into the city, undetected.

Her parents would be around here somewhere. They'd lived fairly close to the wall, unless of course they'd moved into that house they'd looked around. There was every chance that could have happened by now. She didn't quite know how to feel about that. Instead, she occupied her mind by trying to visualise whereabouts in the city she was. She'd lived in the city for over sixteen years, so she had a fairly reliable mental map of the place.

If she remembered correctly, the gate opened up straight into one of the main restaurant districts. Tall wooden skyscrapers lined either side of a narrow, winding, cobbled road. Two tracks down the middle allowed the city tram to roll through every few minutes. The tram was how she used to get to school. It felt like an eternity ago.

The muffled noise from outside her suitcase confirmed it was the morning rush hour. Commuters generally lived above the restaurants, the houses themselves stacked up in a messy wooden web. In the city, builders dealt in space rather than land, so most of the skyscrapers looked like a patchwork of buildings. Some stories looked out of place with the ones immediately above and below, some were jutting out into the street, and others were only staying upright because they were leaning precariously against the neighbouring skyscraper.

When she was little, she'd wanted to live right in a penthouse at the very top, after all, that was where the rich lived, but now the thought nauseated her further. The restaurants below were likely packed with people, eager for an early morning cup of meyacot to get them through the day. She always made it a challenge for herself to not cough on the way to and from school but had never succeeded. Now, trapped in her disgusting prison of bovine fur, it wasn't worth the small victory. Leira wondered if the Luminons had finished lighting the street for the night. It was about the right time for them to retire and go to their home, wherever it was. Leira loved the way they floated and flickered around in their transparent black lanterns, hanging from the buildings. She loved the streams of light that connected them when they wanted to visit or talk to each other, forming glowing, weightless bridges over a road-chasm of smoke and darkness. She wished she was a Luminon.

The city was very beautiful in Leira's mind, but it cast such a dark shadow of memories it was hard for her to appreciate it. Everything it represented Leira despised, and now, being back here, she only wanted to leave.

Finally, the mechanical horse came to a halt. She thought about getting out. It would be such a relief to come out of hiding, to reveal herself to Holliday and for him to just hug her for several hours. She simply couldn't risk any Blue Guard being there though.

Suddenly, the suitcase dropped to the floor, Leira's heart skipping a beat as it fell through the air for just a fraction of a second. She bit her lip to prevent herself from making a noise. If the rest of the journey went like this, her skin would end up being the same colour as her hair...

#

The tram hurtled around the corner at a 45-degree angle, past the city gates and onto the main street. As usual, Conductor Sherwin held onto the railing with one hand and her cap with the other. She'd been working the tram for half her life now and hadn't lost it yet. Today was not the day. Her dark, sun-kissed face lit up with glee as she noticed a total of three travellers queuing up at the stop ahead. *Three more sales, three more tickets.* That was until she noticed the cowboy at the back with four extremely large suitcases that she was going to have to help him lift on board. Well, she'd do whatever it took to get that ticket!

Anyone who hadn't met Sherwin before would be forgiven for thinking it wasn't possible to be passionate about tram tickets, but Sherwin had gained a reputation for asking her customers to hand in theirs at the end of their journey, not so that they could reuse them for other passengers, but so that she could stick them up around her bedroom. For some reason, they were the only thing that helped her get to sleep at night.

With her left foot, Sherwin kicked over the lever to engage the brakes, promptly causing the tram to judder to a halt in a flurry of sparks and a screech of metallic friction. She jumped down and twisted around the printing machine that was slung around her neck proceeding to take the details of each of her customers' journeys:

Abbot's Corner, return.

City Square, return.

Finally, she came to the cowboy. The Stetson and the bandolier of medical supplies were certainly distinctive. She waited patiently as he cut down his suitcases from his clockwork horse and parked it at the stables behind the tram stop, feeding 12 Honeywax into the parking meter.

'And where be you going today, my lurv?' she asked him with a gleam in her eye before typing in the final ticket: *Harbourside, one-way.*

'Return be cheaper than two singles, ya know,' she informed him.

'I ain't coming back anytime soon,' he informed her.

The printing machine whirred as it produced the small piece of paper with the journey details on it before Sherwin ripped it out and handed it to the cowboy. Together, they struggled to get each of the four suitcases up the small step and onto the tram, resorting to the two of them pushing up on the last one in order to fight against its gravity. When they were finally on board and secured, the cowboy stared at his cases, looking confused.

'Forgot something, mister?' asked a completely out of breath Sherwin, as if she could do something about it if he had.

'Naw, naw. Just, I expected one to be a lil' lighter is all. I must be gettin' weaker in ma old age,' he joked, hardly out of breath and hardly over forty.

Sherwin smiled at him and showed him to a seat before walking to the other end of the tram and pulling the brake lever up. With a speed increase over time ratio much higher than it should have been, the tram trundled off down the street and into the heart of the city.

Eventually, the scent of smoke and meyacot gave way to salt and sea and the sound of seahawks tweeting. Over the course of the journey, the tram had lost most of its passengers throughout the city and Sherwin had gained a healthy compliment of tickets to stick up on her bedroom wall, stuffed secretly and securely in her bulging left pocket. Strictly speaking, she wasn't supposed to keep them at all.

There was only one remaining passenger, who remained stubbornly seated until the last stop. Sherwin had kept an eye on the cowboy doctor, not because she was suspicious, but simply because he was interesting to look at. She couldn't decide if that was a good or a bad thing. He was even odder to watch. She could have sworn at one point early on in the journey she'd watched him have a full-on argument with one of his suitcases. That was weird, even for her. He'd seemed incredibly paranoid after that argument, constantly looking out of the window as if someone had been following him.

As she kicked over the lever to engage the brakes, bringing the tram to its final stop of the day before it was to return to the depot, the cowboy finally stood up to collect his suitcases and lined them up at the edge.

'Well sir, 'ere we are. The harbour,' said Sherwin, staring over the sea wall, between the boats and out into the endless ocean. 'Are you staying at The Old Tuning Fork, mister?'

'Why as a matter of fact, I am.'

'Well, it's right over there my lurv,' she said, pointing at the leaning black and white tavern on the other side of the cobbled road. 'Want some help getting your bags down?'

The cowboy nodded and pointed her to the two suitcases on the left. She noted that he had selected the suitcase that he'd had the argument with and took extra care in moving that one down to the ground. Clearly, the suitcase had won the argument.

After struggling to push the two she'd agreed to push to the ground, she took a moment to catch her breath and then held her hand out to the cowboy, indicating that he should hand her his ticket. A little bit confused, but without complaining, he handed it over to her. The cowboy made his way towards his destination and for a moment she considered following him. *What sort of adventures is he going on, and could I be missing out on something?* Sherwin decided that whatever he was doing, it probably didn't involve any forms of public transport. Not willing to put her life of ticket-collecting at risk, she hopped back aboard her tram and rattled away with a fresh new wall decoration burning a hole in her pocket.

#

To his left, the sea wall separated Holliday from the ocean where a veritable consortium of ships waited patiently for their captains and owners to return, with boardwalks forming a maze of bridges between them. To his right, a fellowship of buildings formed the promenade of hotels, taverns, cafés, restaurants and shops, most closed for siesta. The nearest had a little board hanging from the window, which depicted a two-pronged metal device, vibrating after striking an empty glass mug. Holliday wasn't musical, but it was the hotel that Galileo had booked for him and was apparently one of his favourites. At least he was sure to have a good view of the harbour.

It was sights like these that made Holliday wonder if he'd ever return to the city. Generally, the Blue Guard tried to stop people from the desert towns returning, but it was easy enough to dodge the patrols with either stealth or wealth. The public perception of the people who populated the towns wasn't positive. It was a good thing they didn't have a little more intelligence, or else they'd realise that half the people they were looking for over the years had escaped to them.

He could never return though. The people of Runaway needed him. There was such a sense of community and loyalty in the town that he didn't get in the city. Even now, with the prettiest of views by his side, the atmosphere was too busy and hostile for him.

One by one, Holliday wheeled his cases across the tram tracks and towards his hotel.

Once he'd checked in, found his room and taken a moment to catch his breath after carrying four heavy suitcases up a flight of stairs, he unzipped the heaviest one. Instantly, Leira rolled out and crashed to the floor, the black and blue of her hair splayed over the uncomfortable wooden floorboards. Leira took long, deep breaths, only pausing to cough and wretch. She turned around to look back up at him with big, watering eyes. It could have been the sadness, or just the claustrophobia from being in the dingy suitcase for most of the day, he wasn't sure. He stared back down at her.

'You shouldn't have left Runaway.'

He held out a hand to help her up, but she stared at it, instead opting to stubbornly remain on the floor. She twisted herself to face downwards, the visuals of the uninteresting floor perhaps more familiar to her after the excitement of the underside of Holliday's table and the inside of his suitcase. He imagined she was trying to cry into the gaps between the wooden boards, but her tear ducts appeared to have temporarily ceased to function.

'I'm sorry, my girl.'

He fetched her a glass of water as she slowly repeated what had happened since he'd left Runaway, from being hunted down by the Blue Guard and Eliza's death to the entire town being purged. It was a hauntingly similar and yet an infinitely worse horror story to the first one she'd told him when they'd first met. With every word she said, Holliday felt a sear through his heart as if her syllables were being shot through him with a bow. He wanted to console her, but words escaped him. Holliday could only feel disappointed in himself at having let the girl down. As far as he was concerned, he'd failed to look after her, failed to look after Runaway, and she'd paid for it, although he had no idea there was nothing he could have done to stop the attack. If he'd been there, he too would surely be dead. He considered joining her on the floor. His intact tear ducts could easily substitute for hers, but that would help neither of them. Instead, he knelt down beside her and brought her head into his arms.

'I'm sorry, it was worth a try,' mumbled Leira.

'Huh?'

'That's what she said to me. To tell you.'

Holliday's heart tore even further at hearing Eliza's last words. He hugged Leira tighter. He knew what they meant. It was so much like her to spend her last moments protecting the newest runaway. That was what Runaway meant: being loyal to those who are running away with you. They'd put so much effort into protecting those people. They'd failed, but it was worth it. That's what she meant. It wasn't just an apology, it was an instruction. He'd spent his whole time in the town looking up to Eliza, and now was his chance to live up to her standards. This was how he'd remember her.

'My girl, I promise I'll never leave you again. Not whilst you needs me, and not whilst I needs you. We'll travel together, in Eliza's honour. In honour of Runaway.'

They stayed like that, her head on his shoulder, his hands brushing her bright blue and black hair until dusk.

Eight – Shove. Gasp.

The sound of feedback drowned out the tweeting of the seahawks on the harbourside. It was the evening before the launch of Rocket's ship, the Leisurely Ländler, although if you asked Galileo, he would say the ship was his own. They silently agreed to disagree. A curious crowd had gathered in front of a wooden platform, facing the sea wall. Most of them had diverted from the market to the pier, so the air smelled of sour butter-biscuits and glazed rum-buns. People who wondered why there was a crowd joined the crowd to see why there was a crowd, which was really the only reason the crowd was there in the first place.

At the bottom of the platform, by the uneven wooden stairs, stood a woman in a rusty red leather waistcoat and black trousers that were way too long for her. Vale's trademark red cap was stuffed into her pocket to prevent it from blowing off in the sea breeze, instead allowing her long black hair to blow about in front of her face. Every few seconds, she would scrape it off her cheeks with progressively more aggressive scrapes. She turned down the volume on the wood-panelled speaker that was emitting the horrendous feedback sound, much to the approval of the crowd. Whilst she was waiting, she took pictures of the crowd; *the perfect prologue to an around-the-world pro-blog.* She walked up a single step so that she was slightly higher than the crowd and tried to get some shots looking back down the alley. From there, she could see how many people there were. Hundreds and hundreds by now.

Unbeknownst to Vale and hidden in plain sight stood Mattai Morieux in a long beige trench coat. He needn't have bothered wearing his fake glasses and moustache, but he felt that the extra layer of identity protection safeguarded him from fraud and lies, which, for the most part, they did. He was thirsty for answers after chasing leads at the Astronomers' Guild had led him to a dead end. At this point, he didn't even care about the job, he just wanted to know what Vale was up to. *Why all the suspicion? The mysterious meetings, the tarpaulins, the crowds, the veils?* He *had* to know! He shuffled towards the front of the crowd, watching her as she took pictures, but being careful not to get too close.

At the very front of the crowd stood Veroushka, looking up at her new friend as she took pictures, waiting patiently for the event to commence. She hoped she would be in frame for some of Vale's shots but was probably too small. *Ça ne fait rien.* With careful motions, Veroushka twisted the cap off her wooden thermos and brought it up to her mouth, sipping the hot tea inside carefully. She'd had jasmine tea four times since she'd first tried it at The Canary and it was still her favourite. Even so, it just wasn't the same without a slice of the chef's home-made chocolate matcha cheesecake. She kept forgetting to ask her for a regular supply delivered straight to her home. She'd miss that the most.

Snapping out of the distraction caused by the quality of her tea, Veroushka looked up at the tarpaulin that smoothed the curves of the Leisurely Ländler. She couldn't wait to be aboard, searching the world for people like herself, other marionettes. She'd simply had enough of being treated differently, as anyone would. She didn't have any idea how long she'd had to endure it, not even truly knowing her own age. Despite her endearing positivity and happiness, she longed for somewhere she could truly call home. Hopefully, the Leisurely Ländler would give her that. All her hopes and dreams were under that dark green tarpaulin.

A little way down the street and several feet above it, Holliday and Leira took turns looking through the monocular that Leira had returned to him. They watched the crowd from the window of their room, having heard the kerfuffle from their open window. They were both exhausted and incapable of forming any kind of expression on either of their faces, having drained their allocated quota of emotion for the week. They looked over the crowd and at the covered-up Ländler. If it was to be their home for the foreseeable future, then so be it. At least Leira had Holliday and at least Holliday had Leira. Holliday just hoped the rest of the passengers would be nice enough and let her on board. He wasn't quite sure what they'd do if they didn't. Given his experiences, he wasn't optimistic about the pleasantries of the city people.

Under the covers of the Leisurely Ländler, Galileo waited patiently for Rocket to finally finish tinkering with ~~her~~ his ship. Every time he thought she was done, she would walk past him, look him right in the eye, and work on a different part of the ship as if deliberately wasting time and forcing him to stand in its uncomfortable green aura. Frustrated, Galileo left Rocket to whatever she was doing, lifting up the tarpaulin and ducking underneath it to meet the crowd outside. As desperate as he was to reveal his ship to the awaiting crowd, he was nervous about talking in front of an audience and keen to get it over with.

Once she realised Galileo was gone, Rocket threw down her spanner and ran over to the other side of the ship, intending to follow and stop him if possible. It was way too early to be revealing the Ländler yet. She hadn't even finished installing the loop quantum stabilisers or calibrating the velocity of the engines yet. She was struggling to find the balance between telling Galileo how she'd built ~~his~~ her ship, and letting him imagine that she was following his plan down to the letter.

Around the corner, Sherwin's tram was trundling along its usual route through the city and towards its final stop by the harbour. Up ahead, she spotted a blockage in the tracks, where a curious crowd seemed to be gathering. She was confused. For a moment, she considered joining them to see what they were crowding around for. Since the tram was empty, she leapt for the brake and pulled it, the big machine grinding to a halt just meters before the ocean of people. She hopped down from the platform to the cobbled stone and mulled at the edge, hopping up to see if she could spot anything that would give away what was going on. Not being particularly curious, or one for crowds, Sherwin gave up, turned away and walked off home with her ticket winnings for the day. She'd collect the tram in the morning, if it was still there...

Herb the farmer was in the thick of it. He hated coming into the city because everything was so big. The tall wooden skyscrapers reminded him of the big blades of grass that haunted both his fields and his nightmares. As usual, he'd come to buy a new lawnmower from his usual dealer in the market. None of the others appealed to him. By now, he knew them by name, and she knew him by name. Not that they ever talked anymore. After the thirteenth visit, they'd arranged a monthly subscription service, whereby she would provide a new, sometimes improved model, ready for Herb to pick up. Herb would drop by on the fourth Monday of the month and pay his subscription, taking back the new lawnmower to his fields, where he would inevitably fail in shortening the length of his autumn-burnt blades, only to return the next month to collect the next one in the hopes that it would fare better. The communication-free interaction had been going on for years and suited them both perfectly. Herb was content spending all his time cutting grass and the stall owner was content in exploiting the dubious side of capitalism. Herb still hadn't figured out that there was nothing strange or magical about his field, he just kept getting sold questionable mowers.

Today, however, his routine was interrupted by the iron fist of society. In this case, society was quite literally standing in the way of him and his lawnmowers, several hundreds of them in fact. He angrily fought his way towards the stand, looking in the opposite direction to the platform. He failed to see his tenant as she ran out from under the green tarpaulin, chasing after a young man in a long, brown frock.

After several minutes of pushing and shoving, Herb finally made it to his usual stall only to be greeted with disappointment. It was empty. Or rather, it was full of people, but there was no one looking after it. Herb sighed. All that fighting through the crowd for nothing, and now he had to fight his way back out. But then, out of the corner of his eye, he caught a glimpse of a roll of parchment nailed to the wooden frame of the stall. He forced himself around to the other side, almost knocking over a peculiar man in a long trench coat and a moustache that didn't quite suit his face. Herb tore the parchment from the wood and brought it up to his short-sighted eyes:

Dear Herb,

Left the stall to go find out what all the crowd is about.

There's a new model in the cupboard for you. You know the code.

Ah perfect. His subscription and dignity remained in place. He kneeled down to the wooden doors that formed the entrance to the cupboard and entered the code on the number panel to the side. He slid one door to the left and one to the right, and found himself face to face with a brand, sparkling new mowing machine. It was all his, it was glorious, and now, he just had to work out a way to get it out of the cupboard. He had no idea how it had managed to get itself in there in the first place, given that it was longer than the width of the doors. *Who even designed cupboards whose doors were narrower than their width anyway? What was the point?*

In the end, it took three people helping Herb to extract the object of his desire from its rough wooden cage. Herb and his helping hands fell backwards on top of each other, before the perfect new turf trimmer landed on top of them. Herb quickly held out his hands to catch the machine, protecting it from the rough ground and its premature death.

After getting up and thanking his helpers, he strolled away with his winnings, subscription, dignity and brand-new crop clipper intact.

Rocket found herself face to face with crowds flooding the streets. Galileo stood to her right on top of the platform, talking to them about something she'd no doubt find boring if she was listening. Instead, she stared out over the faces that stared back at the man next to her, all of whom had come to see her ship, she thought. Far down to the right, she could see the crowd surrounding the stalls and several people lying on top of each other, and on top of them, what looked like a lawnmower. *How strange...* It was the random oddities of the city she'd miss the most.

In front of her was Vale, the woman she'd directed to Galileo. She was glad he'd invited her on board, having taken an instant liking to her when she'd turned up at the Ländler a week prior. Vale would provide someone for Rocket to tease. She seemed like fun and would also give her inventions some much-needed publicity.

At the front of the crowd, Rocket saw a small marionette, gleaming away in the sunlight. Like everyone else, the inventor was curious about her. For Rocket, it was a purely scientific curiosity. *How did she function? Where did those strings come from? Was she designed? Created? Invented?* When Galileo had introduced her to Veroushka, she had been taken aback by her charm and optimism. It was impressive, for someone who Rocket imagined was considered *different*. Rocket looked at her, hoping that the marionette would spot her and give her a wave. That painted smile could make anyone happy. She got her wish as the marionette lifted the strings to her left arm up and down. Rocket winked back at her.

Galileo droned on and on. Now he was talking about accurately mapping the world, or something. If he was going to be talking like this for their entire voyage, she would soon regret agreeing to come along in the first place. Something about how great it would be to have a record of all the landmasses, and to finally discover the shape of the world they all lived on. Rocket had just assumed it was triangular, but perhaps it wasn't? Nevertheless, the crowd seemed to be at least somewhat enraptured by Galileo's poetic and enthusiastic speech, much to Rocket's disappointment. Well, she'd have to do something about it wouldn't she? She craved the attention of the crowd.

There was only one thing Rocket could do. It involved the incredibly tempting red lever that beckoned her by Galileo's foot. She knew what it did. She'd put it there. It seemed to stare back at her like a bullfighter taunting a bull. She glanced between Galileo and the lever, knowing she'd have an argument with him to ignore later if she pulled it. She sprinted across the platform behind Galileo, who snapped out of his speech and glanced back to see what was going on, reaching out to stop Rocket the second he realised what she was doing.

'Rocket!' he shouted, tripping over as he tried to chase after her, but it was too late. Rocket smirked a devilish grin as she used both hands to pull the lever. The string it was connected to moved the handles of a pair of scissors, which in turn, cut another piece of string. Being Rocket, she had taken the liberty of also connecting some fireworks up to the lever. They exploded in the sky in a variety of bangs, colours, smells and flavours, the crowd *oohing* and *ahhing* at each one. The ropes holding up the big green tarpaulin fell all around it, landing mostly in the ocean and floating on its surface. Unfortunately, it got caught on one of the masts.

Only half of the ship underneath was actually visible, the green tarpaulin still stubbornly obscuring the part that would have been visible to the crowd. Everybody *awwwed*.

This was it. This was the chance for the attention that Rocket wanted. Rocket climbed up onto the cobbled sea wall and leapt across towards the ship, expertly grasping onto a wooden beam, swinging across it and landing by the helm. She grabbed a cutlass that was hanging in its stand off to the side and swung it around, almost killing herself in the process. With childish glee, Rocket looked to her audience to make sure they were watching her, before dashing off to the rigging, jumping up, grabbing the ropes and climbing quickly as high as she possibly could without losing the attention of the crowd. With one swift slash she released the rest of the tarpaulin, which swiftly fell down to meet its other half in the water below.

The crowd finally noticed the magnificent Leisurely Ländler, beginning a cacophony of applause and shouts and screams and whistles and cheers and a storm of camera flashes. Rocket was euphoric, the ship was her child. Galileo just rolled his eyes, yet again unable to hide his smile—the ship was his life. Vale was proud, the ship was her opportunity. Veroushka was giddy, the ship was her freedom. Holliday and Leira managed to smile at each other, the ship was their hope. To everyone else in the crowd though, it was just an incredibly impressive ship.

Mattai, however, hated it. No wonder the board of the directors at the Astronomers' Guild knew nothing about a space mission with a marionette. *How had he not heard of this?* Although he had no right to be, he was furious that Vale had withheld this information from him. *Why had she not told him of this when he'd been ~~spying on~~ researching her? What was the point of oblivious co-operation otherwise?* Mattai pushed his way through to the front of the crowd, where Vale had turned around to face the ship, trying to work out which angle would best capture its majesty.

Hearing the disturbance in the crowd caused by the shuffling, Vale turned around, face to face with Mattai Morieux, her nemesis. She recognised him even before he took off his fake glasses and moustache. They only served to make him look ridiculous.

'Alright, what's going on?' he demanded, the entire crowd going silent to play witness to this newfound drama. Vale simply smiled down at him from the platform, having mentally played out this scene in her head ever since she'd spotted him spying on her at the guild.

'Ah, Mattai, you made it! Hey, Galileo, it's the one I was telling you about!'

Galileo stepped down to ground level and shook hands with Mattai, who momentarily had forgotten he was supposed to be angry.

'Look… Just tell me what you're up to, okay?'

Once again, Vale ignored the question, instead making her way to the top of the platform, standing at the microphone and addressing it so that her voice was propelled by the speakers across the entire crowd.

'Good day, everyone… I'm Vale,' she said nervously, only just realising the extent of her audience and the volume of her voice. She coughed in the silence. 'I'm the photographer for the…'

Suddenly, Galileo was by her side.

'What are you doing?' he said out of the corner of his mouth. Vale covered the microphone. She held up her other hand to stop him.

'Just, let me.'

Galileo rolled his eyes and sighed. Between Vale and Rocket stealing his thunder, he was starting to regret the whole thing. Vale continued with a nervous quiver in her voice.

'So… I'm the photographer on the ship. The official photographer that is. I'm sure you're all aware of *City, The Curious*, the paper. Well, I'm not working for them. Not whilst they hire people like this!' Vale pointed an accusing finger at Mattai, the nervous quiver slowly disappearing. 'This man is a cheat, a fraud and a liar. He steals other people's works and makes them his own. He manipulates and exploits the people of the city, you! All so he can impress the editors to get a pay rise. He doesn't care about telling you the truth. He doesn't care about showing you new and exciting things. He followed me here today to try and take this job from me and deprive you of the truth.'

Mattai jumped up onto the platform, shoving his rival out of the way with his shoulder and gripping the microphone hard, much to the shock of the crowd.

'It's all lies! She's just jealous that I get paid double the amount of Honeywax!' he revealed. The crowd gasped.

'Too right, I'm jealous! You don't work at all! You steal it all from me and god knows how many other people!' replied Vale, shoving Mattai back again. The crowd gasped.

'I did my research! I know how to get information!' Shove. Gasp.

'You call that research! Espionage, theft, and robbery!' Shove. Gasp.

'It gets results!' Shove. Gasp.

'At what cost? Decent hard-working people out of jobs and the people of the city believing any nonsense you throw at them?'

'Nobody cares about the people of the city, they're stupid and deserve to be exploited! I'm all that matters!'

Got him! thought Vale. Mattai looked around, eyes panic-stricken as he realised where he was and what he'd said. He laughed nervously at a silent crowd before backing off the microphone.

'Just a joke, guys... joking... I was only...'

'You vile, rotten and pathetic...' said Vale, struggling to come up with a suitable word despite having been trained in the art of suitable words. She needn't have bothered anyway. At being insulted, the crowd booed and jeered at Mattai, a smile of relief on Vale's face, having wanted to do that for a very long while. She joined in with the booing, pointing her thumb to the ground and shaking it around, not even angry anymore, just glad to have got the people on her side. For a moment, she felt bad. Had she gone too far? He was her friend. He'd been her best friend. But he'd stalled her life for so many years, it was hard to feel bad for long.

Mattai ran down the wooden steps of the platform, sprinted into the crowd and lost himself completely. He'd gone into that fight without a plan and it had showed. He didn't feel bad about what he'd done, no remorse, nothing. The only thing he'd learnt was that next time he should prepare more.

'Er... Thank you, everyone,' came Galileo's nervous voice over the speakers, not quite sure how to end the reveal after that little spectacle had completely overshadowed the one he'd arranged. He was depressed at the idea that all they might remember would be that fight and not the illuminance that was his ship. The crowd slowly dispersed in every direction. He switched off the microphone and turned to the woman he'd hired as a journalist and photographer for his trip.

'Better now?' he asked, sarcastically, raising his hands at her in frustration. She gave an embarrassed shrug. It wasn't the best impression to give her employer on her first day, and she knew it.

'I'm sorry! I don't know what came over me!' A lie, she'd wanted to do something like that for months. 'I only joined up with you to get back at him, I guess there's no point in my coming along now. You probably want to fire me.' Vale stared at the floor swinging her left foot in front of her right and back again, genuinely concerned for her job and surprised at herself for admitting such vengeful motives. She didn't even know herself if that was the truth or not.

A pair of hands covered in black leather gloves found themselves around her shoulders. Vale turned around to see Rocket smiling at her, the ridiculous childish smile.

'We didn't hire you to get revenge on that piece of garbage, we hired you because we like your style and you take a mean photograph,' she said to her. 'So long as you can still do that, why would we not want you?'

'Because of what I did.'

'I don't believe you only joined for revenge. That's not the woman I drenched last week. And, as far as I know, he ain't coming with us, right Gally?' asked Rocket turning to the astronomer. She only got a mumbled agreement in response.

'So, you'll still have me?'

'Of course!'

Vale flung her arms around Rocket, who just stood there, frozen. Rocket's eyes darted to and from Galileo, looking to him for some advice, but he shrugged having no useful experience on the topic to offer. Eventually, the journalist relinquished her grip, allowing Rocket to breathe normally once more.

'I have so much still to do! Bags to pack, I must dash!' declared Vale. Backing away from Rocket and nearly tripping down the wooden stairs in the process. 'I'll see you tomorrow!'

'See you tomorrow,' replied Rocket as Vale packed up her camera inside the bag that had been leaning against the lower half of the platform. 'If I've finished the ship by then...'

'I hope you're joking,' said Galileo. Rocket just looked at him, always maintaining her air of ambiguous humour that she'd fashioned specifically to annoy Galileo. She subtly turned to Vale to give her a wink so that only she would notice it.

Ecstatic, Vale left the harbourside, took the delayed tram to her home on the 37th floor of a 38-story wooden skyscraper, handed in her ticket to the very strange conductor, processed her photographs, packed some bags, and didn't sleep a wink.

#

It was tomorrow, way too early tomorrow. The harbourside was deserted in all places, apart from the largest ship, now freed of the green tarpaulin. Finally, Galileo was able to stand on the deck and look out over the promenade, unimpeded by the green aura that had been the cause of much stress over the past week.

Rocket's legs stuck out from underneath the wheel, where she lay on a rolling plank, tinkering with its inner workings. To anyone watching her work, it looked like she was turning screws and hammering at random. They'd assume she knew better. Little would they know, she was actually just turning screws and hammering things at random. She didn't know better at all. It would work though, it always did for Rocket. Unless it exploded. That happened too, sometimes. Galileo didn't know how she did it. The one time he'd asked, she'd replied with the theory that an infinite number of rabaroos with an infinite number of tritoscopes and an infinite amount of time would eventually chaintwist an entire boxscape of flampeals. He was fairly sure she was just making up words.

'But we don't have an infinite amount of time, I have a schedule! You don't have a time machine!' he'd argued.

'Or do I?' she'd said.

Galileo approached her, and, as had happened often over the last week, had a conversation with her legs. It was their usual conversation at this hour, him trying to convince her that she should really go home and sleep for the night, her insisting that she'd be absolutely fine, and that sleep was for bronze-fish. Given that it was the night before they were to set sail, he was particularly insistent this time, for fear of having a sleep-deprived captain. Finally giving up, Galileo himself retired, leaving Rocket alone to her work.

As he walked off into the night, Rocket wheeled herself out from under the wheel and watched him, smiling as he did so. *Boy, was he in for a surprise tomorrow.* Although, she had messed with him so often, she wasn't entirely sure he wasn't expecting something to happen anyway. The rest of the passengers certainly wouldn't be expecting it though. She was looking forward to meeting them properly. She'd met Vale, briefly, and was looking forward to teasing her some more. Perhaps she'd make a better target than Galileo, less prone to sulking fits anyhow.

Galileo had introduced her to Veroushka, a small, strange, marionette-type figure who was to be looking for her home. Rocket certainly hoped she could help her find it. She already missed her smile.

Then there was Doc Holliday, a doctor and surgeon from the outskirts of the city, who had contacted him with a generous amount of money, and a request to come along to collect medical supplies for his town. It was enough money that they didn't ask too many questions of him. Rocket couldn't wait to meet him. He seemed like the kind of person that would provide the sort of fun and excitement she'd need on a journey of this length.

Rocket rolled herself back under the wheel and returned to work alone, just how she liked it, looking forward to later that morning.

Nine – In the Manner of...

It was still tomorrow, albeit a little later than before this time, as time usually works. There was still no sign of Veroushka. Galileo was starting to worry about her, regretting having not offered to help transport her luggage to the Leisurely Ländler. Holliday had turned up earlier that morning with three heavy suitcases and one very heavy suitcase that he'd helped move down into his quarters. Veroushka was the only person they were waiting for. Other than that, they were ready to leave. At the helm, Rocket snoozed in her captain's chair with her feet up on the wheel, finally getting some much-needed rest.

Having settled into his room, unpacked his bags and returned topside, Holliday leaned on the railing, staring over the last day of the Beirasmus market with his monocular. Shipping and boating enthusiasts camped outside on the shore, eager to see the Ländler set sail for the first time. Everyone else ignored it, the novelty having worn off the night before.

He panned to the right, observing the promenade. People were boarding other boats, smaller than the Ländler, for fishing trips, harbourside tours and just for the sheer novelty of being on a boat. It was a snowy day, so everyone was outside enjoying the warm weather.

He panned down, towards the campers in front of him. Two young boys held the hands of two women, faces covered with the residue of the babarak candy they'd been eagerly devouring. They shyly waved at Holliday, who smiled and waved back. Two young girls held the hands of two men, faces covered with the residue of chocolate-coated rum-buns they'd been scoffing, no doubt procured from the market. They confidently waved at Holliday, who smiled and waved back.

For a moment, he thought that the girl on the right had a jagged streak of dark-red in her hair, but it was just the reflection from a building. A twinge of guilt shook him as he imagined her future and all the terrible things that would be lying ahead for her, had she had colour in her hair. He shivered, she could only be seven or eight. He imagined her in a few years' time, with the same face of Leira, that constant defeated dejection. Leira, on the other hand, lay asleep in his cabin, safe, for the time being. Although he was afraid to admit it to himself, the girl who had turned up in tears in his surgery only one week before had become his entire purpose. Now that the town of Runaway was gone, he would give his life if it meant keeping her safe. He'd been ignorant of so many bad things in the city until then and this was his way of making up for it. He removed the monocular from his eye, unable to look at them any longer, and turned to Galileo, who was nervously twitching beside a sleeping Rocket. He'd wait until they'd set sail to reveal Leira to him.

'Who we waitin' on, partner?'

'Veroushka. Little marionette person... woman... thing...' Galileo replied, so stressed he could hardly get his words out. 'Listen, keep an eye out would you doc? I don't know where she's got to...'

'Sure thing, buddy,' replied Holliday, returning the eyepiece to his face and his sight to the Beirasmus market. Instantly, he recoiled in horror as he spotted a glimmer of blue making its way towards his end of the port. The pristine flags of the Blue Guard tore through the crowds like shark fins through water. Holliday's heart skipped a beat. To hell with some marionette, they needed to leave, now!

Holliday ran across the ship and up to the helm, where Rocket soundly snored, but to his surprise, Galileo was still looking out towards the market.

'There she is!' he shouted, trying to catch Veroushka's attention as she struggled along the cobbled stone promenade with her single suitcase.

Holliday prodded Rocket and she awoke with a start, falling flat on the deck. She quickly jumped up and grabbed a cutlass from the stand, pointing it threateningly at the cowboy. Holliday surrendered to her reflexes instinctively before she realised what she was doing and put the cutlass down.

'Yes?' asked Rocket.

'How quick can ya set sail, ma'am?' asked Holliday with an audible panic in his tone.

'4.31 seconds.'

'Don't ask questions, just do it. I'll explain why later.'

Rocket nodded, the cowboy having unknowingly tapped into her inner desire for unexpected fun.

During the first second, she grabbed hold of the wheel and spun it to the right, away from the harbour, with one hand. Holliday ran down the wooden stairs, glancing left and right between both Veroushka, now near the gangplank, and the armed Blue Guard who were fast approaching the Ländler through the market.

During the second second, Holliday raised his monocular back to his eye in the direction of the guards, still running to the side of the ship. The clothes of the man he saw were unmistakable. Although he'd never seen him before, the golden cloak and colourful crests were exactly how Leira had described the Šéf to him. He didn't have time to react in this second; that would have to be in the next one. Vale ran over to join Galileo at the edge of the ship, waving down to Veroushka. Rocket, still holding onto the wheel, stretched out to pull up a lever with her spare hand. With all her strength, she released the brake, detaching the metal clamps that were keeping the Ländler tied to the sea wall of the port.

During the third second, the entire ship jolted as the ocean suddenly took the full weight of the ship, the water splashing against its hull. Veroushka was too late to walk across the gangplank. She watched as it fell into the depths of the sea. Vale, realising she would be trapped on land, leaned over the edge and held out a hand for the marionette. Galileo furiously looked to Rocket, who frantically used both hands to spin the wheel. *What did she think she was doing?* Holliday knelt down behind the wooden edge of the ship, under the protective railing. He reached in his holster for his revolver, hoping to take the rapidly approaching Blue Guard by surprise.

During the first tenth of the fourth second, Veroushka jumped as high as she could, one arm outstretched towards Vale, the other desperately clinging onto her suitcase. Rocket pressed a big red button on the control panel to her left. By the second tenth, the Blue Guard had lined up in formation on the other side of the sea wall, the Šéf standing by their side. By the third, Veroushka had grabbed onto Vale's hand and her legs were dangling in mid-air. Holliday leapt up and fired towards where he'd calculated the Blue Guard would most likely be.

The sound of a jet engine starting up in the final hundredth of a second was muffled by Holliday's gunshot. Sliding panels just above the rudder had opened up and flames shot out of it, boiling the water below. Slowly, the Leisurely Ländler moved forwards and they were away.

At the helm, Rocket smiled to herself having matched precisely the time she said she could do it in but continued to focus on her control of the ship and an imminent lift-off.

The Šéf raised his hand and quickly dropped it, screaming out his order at the six-strong squad to fire. A hail of bullets riddled port-side. Splinters flew up and nicked Holliday's face, who retreated back below the cover of the railing.

Vale used all her strength to hoist up Veroushka, but struggled. The marionette's suitcase scraped the surface of the ocean below her.

Vale shouted for help to anyone who wasn't preoccupied with their own predicament. Galileo ran over and leant over the edge to see the terrified marionette clinging on for dear life.

As Vale and Galileo carefully swapped over holding onto Veroushka's arm, Holliday jumped back up and fired at another guard. He didn't care about hitting them, only intending to distract them so that they didn't shoot at the others. He ducked once more as they fired back. Vale slowly lowered herself down the outside, nimbly reaching the level of Veroushka's head.

'Give me your bag!' she shouted at the marionette below her, over the roaring of the engines and blasting of gunfire, trying not to think about the endless ocean right beneath their feet. If she let go now, she would surely take Veroushka with her. With no other option, the marionette used all the strength in her strings to lift the handle of the bag and drop it onto Vale's foot. She hauled herself back up the side of the ship, bringing Veroushka's things to safety with her foot and relieving her of some weight at the same time.

Realising that the ship was getting further and further away, the Šéf told his guards to stand down. He took three steps back and started running full pelt towards the ocean wall. At two steps away, he lifted up his right foot and placed it on top of the wall. Placing all his weight on it, he catapulted himself off the top of the wall and flew through the air, across the water, at tremendous height. He grabbed onto the metal railing on the side of the ship so that he too was clinging on above the water.

At the helm, Rocket still grinned like a madwoman, focusing so much on the control of the ship that she was unaware of the chaos ensuing just meters away. Still gripping tightly onto the wheel, she yanked back as hard as she could, her blonde hair falling down to cover her eyes. She whisked them away as she let her whole body be carried by the wheel that was struggling to remain firmly attached to the wooden deck.

Galileo was terrified to see the water get further and further away from him, accidentally slackening his grip on Veroushka. He lowered himself further over the edge to re-grip.

'Rocket! What have you done?!' he shouted at the inventor, who appeared to be having the time of her life.

'Surprise!' she shouted back, noticing he appeared to be holding desperately onto something. 'Everything okay over there?'

'Oh yeah, fine, just fine!'

The Ländler rose further and further away from the ocean surface, the families of enthusiasts on the promenade in awe of the 300ft ship that was ~~sailing~~ flying above their heads, leaving the tallest of the wooden skyscrapers in its trail.

Struggling against the G-Force, the Šéf pulled himself up to the top of the side of the ship, his vision of the deck obscured by the first layer of warm snow clouds that the ship was now travelling through. To his left, both Vale and Galileo were holding tight onto Veroushka, struggling to pull her up.

The doors to the deck below slammed open. The now wide awake and terrified Leira ran out, her eyes darting around to look for Holliday. The Ländler breached the top of the clouds and flew out into the empty void between the layers. Everyone was too preoccupied to notice the stowaway as she ran for the cowboy and clung onto his legs.

'What's going on?' she shouted to him, despite being centimetres apart.

'I'd say I fought 'em off, but I'm over it!' shouted Holliday at the last remaining runaway. He nodded towards the edge of the ship and they both looked over, seeing specs of vanishing land through gaps in the light grey clouds beneath them and solid wedges of darker clouds above them.

It only took Leira a second to look to the right, and there he was, the man who had made her life hell: the Šéf, climbing his way up the side of the ship and nearly reaching the deck. He dangled from the edge of the Ländler, hair blowing in every direction, golden blue robes threatening to tear themselves away from his body with the wind, as they soared higher and higher through the sky. In that moment he was all that was wrong with the world.

From the corner of her eye, Leira spotted it. Holliday's revolver taunted her from its holster. *Come on, you know what you've got to do.* It beckoned her to take it. She swiftly manoeuvred her arm around and grabbed it with her hand, pulling it up out of the holster, throwing it up in the air, spinning it around and catching the base, aiming it straight at her target. Holliday had taught her that one. With her arm fully outstretched and a finger on the trigger, she stormed over to where the Šéf was, a burning fire of rage in her eyes. In that moment, it was only the two of them, and she owned him. She stared at his pathetic face through the sights of Holliday's gun and he stared back at her up the barrel, his eyes begging for mercy.

Leira stood her ground, not backing down, lifting back the hammer and gritting her teeth as she stopped less than a meter away from where he was hanging, seething and heavily breathing, hearing only her own heartbeat above the racket of the engines. Nobody could stop her. Galileo and Vale were too busy desperately hauling up the marionette. Rocket at the helm was busy trying to control the turbulence and Holliday was conflicted as to whether or not he should, knowing full well what she'd been through. She willed herself to murder him. Time and chaos seemed to freeze around her.

Suddenly, darkness.

The entire Ländler entered the thicker second layer of cloud, obscuring all vision completely. The ship shook violently with the turbulence, throwing Leira to the hard-wooden deck and Rocket over her wheel. The Šéf's left hand could hold on no more. Now, with only a single limb connecting his body to the safety of the Ländler, he attempted to twist and turn his body to try and regain some kind of stability. Vale and Galileo looked down simultaneously, only aware that they were still hanging onto Veroushka from the weight. Leira scrambled back upright.

Suddenly, brightness.

The entire Ländler bathed in the glow of the sun, unimpeded by the opaque clouds that had been blocking it. The Šéf was blinded! He released his remaining hand from its hold in an attempt to shield his eyes from the intense, burning light. In a moment of empathy, Leira snapped out her arm in an attempt to save the man she had wanted to kill, but it was far too late. She leant over the edge, watching, as the Šéf flailed through the air and finally disappeared beneath the dark second layer of the clouds, hopefully, gone from her sight forever.

Finally, Rocket stabilised and the Leisurely Ländler levelled out. No longer fighting the forces of nature, Vale and Galileo used their remaining strength to bring a poor, terrified Veroushka onto the safety of the deck. She fell into Vale's arms and held onto her tightly, not daring to look behind at where she'd come from. Vale rested her cheek down on the marionette's woollen hair and gently stroked her wooden face. For Vale, the wooden crinkles of the rough texture felt like bony veins. All her knowledge was telling her that Veroushka should not be possible, but the receptors on the ends of her fingers were telling her that she was very much alive. In that moment, she forgot everything about her journalistic instincts and was left with compassion.

Although the marionette had no receptors on her fingers, or anywhere in fact, the hug was still comforting, the touch of another being that she felt so rarely made her feel warm, regardless of her lack of ability to physically feel.

Leira felt another hand on her shoulder as she peered over the edge. Now, there was only one hand that was acceptable to be there, and she turned to see it. Holliday turned her around to face him and looked her in the eye.

'Couldn't do it, could ya?' he asked, undecided if he was proud or disappointed, possibly a bit of both. She shook her head and turned around the revolver, placing it in Holliday's outstretched hand. 'Then you're better than him. And, you're a hell of a lot better than me.' He holstered the weapon.

Leira had had him entirely at her mercy. It wasn't like the Blue Guard she'd killed in the firestorm, that had happened so fast and that forced her to protect herself. Here, it felt like time had stopped and she'd had to make the decision. This would have been homicide as a choice. Like she'd been doing so many times over the last week, she replayed the scenes in her mind. She'd felt so powerful in that moment, but genuinely didn't know if she would have done it. Holliday had certainly prepared her to, but in that moment, she had hesitated, and Rocket and her terrible piloting had made the decision for her. Eliza was right, those who enjoy their power don't deserve it.

However, she was content that Holliday thought she'd made the decision herself and hoped that she'd never be tested on her morality again. She jumped up and wrapped her arms around his head, forcing him down to meet her in a hug. He gently wrapped his arms around her as he knelt down to her level.

'Hey! Look!' shouted Rocket as the engines slowly settled at a quieter velocity, the Ländler beginning to gently settle down into a cruise through the sky. The two groups of hugging explorers turned to look at their captain in unison. She was pointing up and around them. Their eyes followed her arms and were met with a glorious sight. Giant majestic birds swam and soared above and around them, the likes of which had only been witnessed through a telescope. Galileo marvelled at their true size.

Holliday relinquished Leira and ran for the edge to the left. He grabbed onto the metal rail, leaned over and let out an almighty 'Yee-haw!'. Finally, they were able to appreciate where they were, and how far each of them had come, even having only just set off.

Vale relinquished Veroushka, grabbed her hand and dragged her to the right of the ship. Finally, they had escaped from the toxicity of the city. Vale from the jealousy of her nemesis and Veroushka from discriminatory paranoia.

Rocket gently adjusted the wheel and pulled down on the throttle to a leisurely glide. She was finally getting used to controlling her creation. Galileo walked up to the helm and stood next to her, not even bothering to pretend to be angry this time. He smiled at her.

'I hate you,' he stated with a huge grin. Rocket stared back, knowing that he didn't. She smiled back at him, wide-eyed and crazy-faced.

'Where to first, friend?' she asked.

'Onwards?'

'That doesn't actually help me, you know, I can't just navigate to… onwards…'

'I said, onwards.'

Rocket sighed. 'Onwards.'

#

The sombre and sentimental sight of the silver sunset was certainly something as it sank south of the second layer of clouds. Nobody had seen anything like it before, at least, not from this angle. But now, as Vale took picture after picture from the top of the deck, she couldn't help but be somewhat proud of herself. This was exactly what she had joined them for. She was ecstatic just to be there.

The air and atmosphere were calm. Finally, the newly formed team of explorer's had a chance to relax. Doc Holliday had set up a small round table on the quarterdeck so that Rocket, Galileo, and himself could play a game of clockwork poker. The captain leant on the back two legs of her chair and held the wheel steady with her tightly booted feet. She peeked at her cards and squirmed. Holliday carefully analysed her face, looking for a tell. *Was she bluffing, or did she have nothing? What was that expression?* He guessed bluff and moved a few of his chips over to the middle of the table, keeping as straight a face as possible.

Galileo's turn. After careful consideration and going through every possible play in logical order, he matched the bet, counting out his chips and placing them in the middle with a defeated sigh. After losing several rounds, he was starting to hate this game. It just wasn't logical to him, and he could never tell the expressions on his companions' faces. Next, it was Rocket's turn. She instantly shoved her entire stack of chips into the middle, much to the horror of her two opponents. Holliday stuck with his decision, shoving his entire stack into the pot also. Galileo angrily flipped over his cards and leaned back in his chair, revealing his Elephant of Spanners and Weasel of Cogs. His eyes watered, he looked like he was about to cry, but was desperately trying to hide it. He caught Holliday looking at him sympathetically and turned to face away, but, deciding it wasn't enough, he got up and sulked over to the opposite end of the ship.

Only Rocket and Holliday remained in the hand, both all in. He stared at her like he'd stared at the bandits in the showdown last week, this time with a glimmer in his eye. She turned over her cards one at a time. Ace of Hammers and Ace of Drills. She smirked at him, proud of her 'pocket rockets'. He turned over his cards, revealing a Krokket of Cogs and a Seahawk of Cogs. It was a well-known myth that Rocket got her name due to a low-key obsession with jet engines and explosions. In actual fact, she'd acquired the name due to a remarkable talent for not only being constantly dealt a pair of aces in clockwork poker, but somehow managing to lose with them every time, despite it being the best possible starting hand. She much preferred the other explanation for her name. As the remaining cards came down her smirk soured, realising that once again she had lived up to her name and lost with pocket rockets. Frustrated, she moved her legs down from the wheel, got out of her chair which promptly fell over, and went back to furiously press some buttons that she'd put on the main control panel for no reason other than for anger management.

Leira had never been more nervous than when she'd watched Holliday explain to Rocket and Galileo why she was there. She could feel all the eyes staring at her, like she was being judged. Even so, they'd accepted her.

'Even if we didn't want you, we could hardly turn back and drop you off!' Galileo had joked.

Still, she had her doubts about the ship. It still felt *wrong,* although no more wrong than her home in the city had. For now, however, it would do. Perhaps somewhere on their travels it would feel right. Only time would tell.

She sat on deck, perched on a wooden beam, looking down on Veroushka, who, because she didn't need to sleep, had kindly offered that Leira could stay in her room.

'So, why are you here?' she asked the marionette.

Veroushka looked up at the sweet girl, a look of confused defeat on her face. Of everyone she'd come across, Leira seemed to treat her with the most respect. Although the rest of the explorer's were kind enough, she always detected a certain level of caution. It was suppressed, but she could tell they thought of her as *different.* After all, she *was* different. Nothing was going to change that, but at least they were trying. She didn't detect any of that from the girl with the blue hair and it wasn't hard for her to guess why.

'I am different, *ma cherie,*' she replied. 'I grow weary of being treated as such. *Oui,* it is as simple as that. I am looking for home.'

'Do you think you'll find it?'

'I know I will. I believe it is my destiny. I don't know what it may be, or when we might find it, or where, but I know that I will find my home.'

Leira didn't believe in destiny, but the infectious confidence of the small marionette made Leira believe in it just for a moment. She managed a tiny smile with the corner of her mouth.

'You are sad, *mademoiselle*?' asked Veroushka. Leira hadn't even realised the drops of tears that had slowly started crawling their way down her cheek. She felt it with her hand and dabbed it off.

'I... I don't know where I'm going, or why I'm here,' she admitted, struggling to use words with her breaking voice. 'I'm not sure I know who I am.'

'You are from the city?'

'Yes, but I don't belong there,' she said realising it was the first time she'd ever admitted that. She paused to look at the marionette. For the first time in a long time, Leira was stunned. Here she was, having a *conversation* with a marionette. There was only one possible question.

'Where are you from?' she asked, trying to be as subtle as possible.

'Ah, I have heard this question many times. But I do not know *mademoiselle*. I was found unconscious on the harbour and made the city my home. I have no memory of my life before this.'

Veroushka appeared wistful, her painted eyebrows at diagonal angles to her eyes pointing up to the sky.

'And that's what you're searching for?' asked Leira.

Veroushka carefully controlled the strings to her left hand and guided it towards Leira's swinging legs. She gently dropped her cold wooden hand onto her knee. Instinctively, Leira backed off, but for once used all her brain strength to decide that she did in fact want it there, moving her legs back towards the marionette.

'Perhaps our destinies lie together?' suggested Veroushka. Leira liked the idea, but doubted it, nonetheless. Being brave, Leira took her own hand and placed it over the marionette's, who gleamed back at her.

Detecting a third presence, both Leira and Veroushka snapped their heads towards Vale, who was standing right beside them with a smile on her face and her camera in her hand.

'Group photo? To celebrate a successful... lift-off?' she suggested as she pointed over to where she had Rocket and Galileo waiting patiently on the poop deck.

'*Zut Alors*! But if Rocket is there, who is flying the ship?' asked Veroushka, concerned for the safety of the Ländler and its new inhabitants.

'It's okay, she has an auto-captain. It's almost as good as Rocket, so I'm told...' said Vale, clearly unsure of the excuse herself. 'Come on!'

Veroushka, excited at finally being able to have her picture taken, began to follow the journalist back towards the end of the ship, but stopped as she realised that Leira was not behind her. She looked at the girl with a puzzled look drawn on her face. She was clearly reluctant to be in front of the camera, but Veroushka insisted, even resorting to gently prodding her legs to get her to come down from the rigging. Leira didn't have the energy to fight back, so she made her way over to join the others for a nice big group photo.

Whilst waiting, Holliday took the opportunity to talk to Galileo, something he'd been trying to do since they'd met. He still seemed upset about the poker game and was unable to look him in the eye as he talked. He didn't seem to like touch, and seemed disturbed by certain things, having avoided touching the first pack of cards due to them being green. Holliday was no expert in psychology, but he'd read about people exhibiting this kind of behaviour before. It wasn't something he'd ever come across, until now. Holliday relished talking to him and attempting to get him to come out of his shell, almost being disappointed that he had to stop the conversation upon the arrival of Leira, Vale and Veroushka. He made a mental note to treat Galileo with care. Rocket was eccentric. But the strange astronomer who dressed like a monk, who was afraid of so much yet had taken so many risks to get this far, was something far more compelling. If he were back in Runaway, he could do a proper diagnosis, but for now, he would have to make do not knowing.

Not used to it being so bright, Vale took longer than usual to get the settings right on her camera, but finally got them as right as possible. She ran in front of the lens to join her fellow explorers in the line, grabbed the button that Rocket had been holding onto for her and made sure that it was connected up properly before counting down.

'One! Two! Three!' they chanted all together.

She pressed the button and in a fraction of a second they were blinded by the flash. Vale ran back to the camera to get an instaprint. She shook it about in the air and looked at it, over the moon at how well it had come out, even for a first copy. Knowing she'd want to see it, she handed the rough print to Veroushka first, who stared at it with her mouth painted gaped. After only ever having seen herself in mirrors, this was a real treat.

'That one's for you!' Vale declared. Veroushka simply didn't have the words, only able to manage a slight increase in breath frequency. She gripped on tight to her print as the others gathered around her to look, every single one of them smiling and pointing out their own ridiculous expressions, of which Rocket's was naturally the most ridiculous.

By now it was late, and the silver sunset had almost completely disappeared. Galileo yawned, loudly and obnoxiously.

'Well, *mes amies*, who would like a cup of tea?' asked Veroushka. 'I'm going to put my kettle on.' Holliday laughed, finding it funny how of all the things she'd needed to pack into her single bag, a kettle had been the priority. It had been a stressful day and a horrifying week, but there was always a cup of tea at the end. It felt like a reward to him. They definitely all deserved it, and the fact that nobody declined confirmed that the others felt the same way. The marionette led the explorers down through the double doors beneath the quarterdeck.

Subtly, Rocket shook her head at Leira and then back towards herself, indicating that she should stay. Confused, she obliged, waiting until it was just the two of them on deck. For the first time in a long time, the crazy inventor was deadly serious.

'Are you okay?' she asked, taking responsibility in her role as captain, but knowing full well there was nothing she could do about it if she wasn't. Holliday had told Rocket, briefly, what she'd been through, omitting any unnecessary detail. Rocket understood of course. Despite her quirky façade, she was socially aware.

'Yes,' lied Leira, knowing full well that her captain could do nothing about it.

'You're safe here and you always will be,' Rocket assured her. 'Well, that is unless I crash the ship into a mountain or something, but I'll try not to do that... promise...'

Leira wanted to smile at her but couldn't bring herself to do it. The inventor was holding out her hand. Leira just looked at it, confused. Did she want her to hold it?

'I hear you have something for me?'

That was just even more confusing! What could she possibly have for the inventor? Her only remaining possession was a broken earpiece. *Wait... broken?* Leira's eyes widened as she realised what Rocket meant. She dashed inside and ran straight for her room, grabbed her golden earpiece by the wing and made her way back outside as fast as she could. When she got back, Rocket was standing in exactly the same position with her hand stretched out, the exact same expression on her face. Leira placed her broken earpiece in her outstretched hand. Rocket wrapped her fingers around it, brought it up to her face to investigate and pocketed it.

'Well, I'm not promising anything, but I'll give it a go!' she said. 'Why don't you go join the others, I'll be along in a bit.' Leira nodded and made her way back indoors leaving Rocket alone with her Leisurely Ländler.

She walked around and up to her place at the helm and put two hands on the wheel. She stood, staring out over the horizon with a euphoric sigh, feeling the material whisk by her skin as the auto-captain turned slightly to the right. She listened as the wind blew between the sails and the hull gently creaked, breaking the silence of the sky.

'We did it, mate,' she told her ship as she patted the wheel and watched as the world flew by around her.

Ten – Coda

T he harbourside bells rang gently in the breeze of the night. With a head full of toxic meyacot and a handful of rum-buns, Lucky Buster stumbled along the promenade, hardly able to see the Luminons that were bridging the gaps between the lampposts. Without them, he would surely stumble headfirst into each and every one of them. The sea wall, however, was not lit up, so he could do nothing to stop himself falling headfirst into its rocky exterior and dropping his remaining snacks onto the snow-covered floor. *Just great!* he thought to himself as he resigned himself to the fate of his food. There he sat, feeling sorry for himself. At least there was no-one around here to see him in this state. He slumped to the ground, too delirious to notice the warm water seeping up through his torn clothes, dampening his skin. Lucky let his body soak it up.

And there he sat for an hour until finally he fell asleep, at least, until the sound of splashing water behind him woke him up. He scrambled up, balancing himself on the cobbled wall and flicking his dreadlocks out of his face in an attempt to see properly through the snowstorm.

'Hello? Someone 'ere?' he shouted out into the vast dark expanse of the ocean in the vague direction of the disturbance. He couldn't be sure, but it definitely looked like a figure swimming towards the shore at impressive speed. Lucky stood, watching with his mouth wide open, trying to process the situation and analyse the figure that, he could only assume, was now climbing up the opposite side of the sea wall.

The dripping wet figure sat on top of the wall with its head in its hands. What had clearly once been a robe of rich majesty, covered with jewels and sequins, was now devoid of decoration, likely having been ripped off by the cruel forces of the water.

'Are y'okay?' asked Lucky.

The man ignored him, instead rolling up his golden robe by his legs and squeezing out the water onto the floor beside him. Lucky sidestepped to avoid the splashback. The man rolled down his crinkled robe, quickly, as if trying to hide what was underneath, but it was too late. Lucky had already seen the spinning cogs and wheels of a clockwork leg in between the gaps of the man's skin, engraved with a strange 'R' symbol that meant nothing to him. He blinked twice, quickly. He *must* be hallucinating.

'Are y'okay?' asked Lucky again, forgetting he'd asked that a moment ago. Remembering more than ten seconds ago was difficult. The man from the ocean rolled his eyes.

'Tell me, how far would you go for the wealth and prosperity of the city?' asked the man. Lucky looked at him, confused. It was an odd question, one that he'd never really thought about. He considered himself, broke, lodgingless and alone. How far would Lucky Buster, the once famous fighter, go to live up to his name again? He'd read the stories in *City, The Curious* about how the city used to be. Would he be where he was now in a city like that? How many other people like him would be better off in a city like that? Having made up his mind, he replied:

'Me, sir? I'd do anything, I would, anything at all. For the city or m'self,' he said confidently. Lucky considered who was asking him, probably something he should have done earlier. He looked important, but what had he been doing swimming in the sea? Perhaps he actually had the power to make the city wealthy and prosperous again. The ocean man laughed a singular snarling laugh at his response.

'Me too,' replied the man. 'If the city would let me.' He hopped down from the wall and stumbled over on his metal leg as if it had seized up from the water. Lucky rushed over to help stabilise him. 'Thank you. What's your name, friend?'

'Lucky, sir. Lucky Buster.'

With one arm around him, the man looked Lucky right in the eye.

'Well, Lucky Buster, this might just be your lucky day,' he said with a hearty chuckle. Lucky didn't understand what was so funny.

With that, Lucky and his new friend walked into the night. In that moment, he didn't know where they were going. He and the man from the water were just wandering around aimlessly, but for the first time in a long time, Lucky Buster had a new destination.

Delia Simpson

About the Author

Born and raised in Leeds, Delia currently works as a software developer. Apart from writing, she enjoys composing music and playing video games.

Having had very little interest in reading since she was a child (she knows this is heresy), her stories are inspired mostly by old fantasy and sci-fi shows so has not written much prose. As such, she is not very good at writing bios within the character limi

Printed in Poland
by Amazon Fulfillment
Poland Sp. z o.o., Wrocław

59891305R00089